Mine to Fear

Book Three
by
Janeal Falor

To learn more about this author, please visit: www.janealfalor.com

Cover Art by Rainbow Danger Designs

For Michelle
An awesome editor
and an even better cousin

CHAPTER 1

Waverly

Being in Envado when those I care for the most are stuck in Chardonia makes me want to spit. What terrors are befalling them while I'm here, unable do anything to help? Cynthia is being hidden by our rebel group. Serena is living alone, away from her sisters and mother who are once again owned by her father.

I'd like to think at least my brother Zade and Serena are happy now that they're engaged, but knowing they could have gotten engaged just a little sooner while I was there to witness it? It makes me want to spit again. And to make things even worse, Zade's previous fiancée arrived here for a visit this morning. Unfortunately, I did witness her engagement, which makes it all the more awkward.

What's worse is that Zade's previous fiancée doesn't know about Serena and Zade. I need to tell her that he chose a girl Zade formally owned over her. He didn't just give Serena her freedom, but he gave her his heart. While the two fell in love, Cynthia proved to everyone at the tournament she can do magic, and do it well. Maybe it'd be easier if I wasn't such close friends with both

Serena and Zade's previous fiance. It's dreadful this is much too formal of a setting as my mother's entertaining room to spit. Plus, my mother is here, and she wouldn't put up with it.

"I'm so glad you came to visit." The words are true enough, though they would be even more heartfelt if she already knew about the engagement.

"I should have come sooner," Tawny says. "I'd like to use my duties as an excuse for not coming, but really, I just didn't know how long it would take you to adjust to returning home. With the things they say about Chardonia it must be a challenge."

I'll never adjust. This no longer feels like home, even though it's safer.

"It was very thoughtful of you to take time away, Tawny." Mom fills my silence, pouring sincerity into her words. Since my return from Chardonia last week, she knows what a pest I have been.

"How was Chardonia?" Tawny's question is sure to make Mother cringe inside, even if she doesn't show it. "Were the men as bad as everyone says?"

"No. They were worse." Which is why I should be there, helping, instead of here having tea and biscuits in a room with pictures spelled with sparkles and a floor spelled to stay cushioned and warm.

"Will you tell me about it?" Tawny presses.

She's just like everyone else who's paraded through our entertaining room since my return, all wanting to know the gossip from Chardonia. Politicians wanting to know the state of the government, women wanting to know how much better off we are, men wanting to know how other men really behave, shop owners trying to see if there's any news on trade. All wanting something for themselves.

Except Tawny. She seems different, even if her question is the same. There's a glint in her eyes as she holds herself as if ready to jump up for a fight instead of leaning in to pick up every word to pass onto others. It would be like her. She always was ready to take action when others just wanted to talk. Perhaps it's time to really tell someone about what things are like. Lands know I'm well past wanting to.

"Mom, would you mind asking Cook to make those new treats she's learned? I'm sure Tawny would love to try them."

"Wonderful idea, dear. I need to check on your father anyway." She brushes a kiss to my forehead, something she's done much more often since my return. "I'll see you again soon, Tawny. Send your mother my regards."

"I will."

Once the door closes behind my mom, I grin at Tawny. "Mom always did like you."

"I think she's still hoping Zade will come back for me."

Discussing the state of Chardonia is much more preferable to this. "And is that what you want?"

She looks at her hands. "I don't know. We grew up together. We always thought we were destined to be married. It's almost expected. But since he wrote to break off the engagement... Mom isn't taking it well. Dad seems to have expected it, though."

That doesn't answer my question about her, though. It's the perfect time to tell her about Zade's engagement. "Chardonians are horrid," tumbles out instead.

"How so?"

"The warlocks treat the women worse than animals and those who have been tarnished, people who are spelled to be bald, inked, and barren. Then the women who they want to discard or men that have little to no magic, are taught to believe they aren't even people. They're just tools with brains."

"Could you do anything to help?" Her eyes grow bright with interest.

"Not nearly enough." The words feel so good to get out. "Just trying to get the women to understand their worth was a chore. I wish I was still there helping them figure it out."

"It does sound like something worth doing." She glances up

3

shyly and in a whisper says, "Something I'd like to help with. Not just here yammering about things, but over there making a difference."

Shock courses through me. I would have never guessed she would have an interest in such things. "Would you truly?"

"I would."

The room is silent as I think about that. What would Tawny's parents say? Her mother, the Queen, would likely not want her daughter, the third in line for the throne, in harm's way. It would probably be my head on the chopping block since I brought the idea back with me from Chardonia.

Tawny breaks the silence. "Mother wanted to make certain your family got the invite to the ball this evening."

I'm still lost on the idea of her wanting to help in Chardonia. Mother would want me to accept the invitation even though I'd rather stay home and father is still too weak to leave. "Thank you. We did and would be delighted to attend."

* * *

After Tawny leaves, I remain in the sitting room staring at nothing, wondering what to do, if anything, about Tawny's declaration. Not that I can even be in Chardonia like I want to, though, so I don't know why I'm contemplating anything to do with her declaration. There's no way she could go. Besides, Zade would have my head.

"Are you pining for Chardonia or for Chadwick?" Mom's question startles me from the thought.

"That's not even a question."

"Both then?"

I don't have the heart to tell her it's definitely only one. Though I do miss Chadwick, it's not the way she means. At least I don't think it is...

"I accepted the invitation to the Queen's ball this evening," I say.

"Oh good. It's been too long since Queen Brundy and I chatted. When I saw Tawny, I was hoping her mother had joined her. I suppose she's busy with government, especially with all the growing political problems with Chardonia."

"I'm certain she is." New rumors spread everyday, and it quickly feels like I've lost touch with those I care about. The border closures are getting tighter. The watching, even the lower class, is stricter. The hunt for the rebels is vigorous. There hasn't even been word from Cynthia. Why hasn't she spelled me a message to let me know if she's safe? Have they caught her and Lukas?

As I enter my room, it just makes me long for a room back in Chardonia, whether one of the cramped ones or big, it wouldn't matter. At least in Chardonia I was not only helping but I gained freedom from the expectations set on me here in Envado. Of marrying and becoming a woman of taste and elegance. Of course, those expectations are nothing compared to what the women in Chardonia face, and they still don't even realize how bad it is. The horrors of being beaten and hexed by men who owned them. If I could bring them all here for a month, maybe then they'd begin to understand.

Going there was the best choice I ever made. After Zade freed Serena and Cynthia showed everyone that women could not only do magic but win the entire tournament with it—me doing a few magic spells when no one was looking and helping with simple chores there doesn't seem like enough. I want to be more. I want to do more. I want to make a difference.

Instead, I'm going to a ball.

Gee, what good am I doing? If only Sanos, the rebel group secretly aiding Chardonia, would have let me help. They should have at least sought my opinions instead of just rumor digging like everyone else. If only they didn't see me as a liability because I wasn't as trained as they were, thanks to Zade and Chadwick trying to protect me. I shouldn't be home while they're in Chardonia helping. Just thinking of it makes me wish Zade was around to argue with.

I still can't believe they sent me home.

CHAPTER 2

The ball is more lavish than others I remember attending. Spells are everywhere, sparkling, dancing, swishing across the room in the form of birds and butterflies. Drinks are flaring up like fireworks. Dresses are changing colors and styles. Men's suits are too. It used to impress me, but now it's a waste. Don't these people realize what's going on just across the border?

Apparently not.

A woman approaches mother and me, hair spelled bright fuchsia, twisted up too high atop her head with pink and purple spelled butterflies flitting around it. Her dress is spelled to sparkle in time with the music, and her make-up changes every few seconds, each time to something more gaudy than the last. "Waverly, you're back! Are you going to hold a party soon? No one throws parties as grand as yours."

I make some excuse, but my thoughts are on the parties I held. Is she right? Were they really more garish than this? What type of example did I set? The thought sends my stomach churning as I disengage from the woman. Who did I used to be? When did I change?

I want to be back at home, and my mom knows it.

Mom pulls me forward. "We have to greet the Queen at the very least. It would be rude to leave before then."

It's true, but being here has only made me more frustrated with the frivolous behaviors of my fellow countrymen when there are women who can't breathe without their husbands' permission back in Chardonia. The way everyone here flitters about without a care, or at least cares that aren't life-threatening, drinking and talking and casually casting their spells, makes me long for a place that actually needs my help. Or someone to punch.

When I don't respond to mother's statement, she says, "I'm worried about you. Nothing has been the same since you came home."

Nothing seems the same as it did before.

"I thought this ball might cheer you up. You always loved them before," she says. "When you told me you accepted the invitation, I thought it might be the opportunity you needed to return to your old self. I think I was wrong, though. Not just about the ball but about more. This feeling, and the way you've been since coming home, it goes deeper than socializing, doesn't it?"

I wave randomly around the room. "All this, everyone here, all the spells and extravagant things? It seems wasteful after living with women who can't even go out in public without a male chaperone. Who can't even make their own choices without being punished because of them." And I need to get back to where I can do some good. How do I convince my parents of that?

"I suppose living in Chardonia would change how you see things." Her shoulders slouch like the weight on them is growing too heavy. She has enough to worry about with Dad and Zade. I shouldn't add to it. I'm just so restless, and the words keep popping out.

"It has changed everything," I say.

She dabs her eyes with her kerchief even though there's no sign of tears. "Honestly, with your dad feeling so sick when we left, I'm not of the mind for this type of thing anyway. Let's pay our respects to the Queen and King and return home."

"Thank you."

As we make our way toward the thrones, another woman stops me. "You're Waverly, yes?"

"I am."

"It's such an honor to meet you. I've heard all about everything you've done for Chardonian women."

Oh, she has, has she? It's funny that she knows more than I've told anyone. Someone in Sanos, the rebel group, must have been talking, but even they don't know *everything*.

"You're held in such high esteem," the woman continues. "What, with helping the first woman to duel in the Chardonian tournament."

This is ridiculous. I did so little, and everything they think they know about what I did is just a rumor. They have no idea what it's really like. I've heard more than enough. "I did nothing but teach her to make bubbles and color nails."

I storm away from the woman, fuming as I head toward the Queen. What an inane country I belong to. They claim to want to help the Chardonian women, yet all they do is parade around in the spelled finery. No, I want out. I'm needed out there.

* * *

MOM PARKS THE MOTOR CAR.

"This is one thing I did miss," I say. "It's such a refreshing change to be able to get places faster. They don't even have windows in their carriages, Mom. And they wouldn't let me ride a horse unless we were hidden from prying eyes."

Mom blanches. "They grow more barbarous every time you say something about them."

She would never survive without her daily horse ride.

"The girls were wonderful, though," I say, trying to point out at

9

least something good since I did nothing but complain about Chardonia on the way home. She's probably sorry Zade didn't send me home sooner, so I'd have less to complain about.

We wander into the house together and head toward the study. "They sound wonderful the way you've described them. It's amazing how they could turn out so good with such terrible surroundings."

I suppose I may have over-talked the girls. Even if I've been hesitant to speak about anything else but Chardonia up until this point, I haven't refrained from telling her all about the girls I now consider my sisters. My heart aches from missing them so much, each and every one of them.

It's too quiet here without the little ones and lonely without the others.

The study is quiet as we enter. Dad is pale and much too thin where he sits near the fire reading. Zade's so much like him, but the resemblance has been worn by sickness. It makes me ache for them both.

"How are you feeling tonight, Daddy?" I place a kiss on his forehead and curl up by his feet.

"Dandy." He does sound better than when I first left for Chardonia. "How is the Queen?"

"As graceful as ever."

Mom sits on the arm of the chair and wraps her arm around Dad's shoulders. Something about the movement reminds me of Zade and Serena, and Lukas and Cynthia. It pierces my heart with longing.

I stand, even though I just got settled. "I think I'll do some reading."

I take a step, but Dad stops me. "Wait a moment, dear. Your mother and I have been talking."

Perfect. The last time they said they'd been talking like this, I ended up cleaning out the horses' stalls for a month. Best nip that. "You've decided to buy me my own motorcar?"

10

"That may actually be preferable to what we've decided."

Lovely.

Mom shifts uncomfortably. It must be worse than I think. I plop down on a nearby chair. "What is it?"

"We're so glad to have you home," she says. "We missed you so very much."

And that's one of the reasons I haven't snuck back to my almost-sister's yet despite the overwhelming desire to run off. "I know."

"But you're not happy," Daddy says.

I force a smile. "I am happy. I missed you both so much."

"But we're not enough. You miss your brother and new friends."

Sigh. "It's not that you two aren't enough. It's only that they need me more."

"We know, and we love you so much. Love having you home, love spending time with you, love only having to worry about the life of one of our children. It's been a good week. But we know there's greater things out there for you." My heart pounds. "This isn't where you want to be, or where you need to be. Zade and Chadwick had good intentions, but they were wrong to send you home."

Are they really saying this? Is this really leading to what I think it is?

"Your notes sounded like things were hard, but you knew how to handle them. How to help your friends and the other Chardonians. To make things better. Without that, well, sweetie, you now seem to be floundering."

"Just look at you," Mom says. "You're already perking up just at the mention of it."

Guilt pricks me at the fact, that this is what makes me happy and not my parents. Despite that, the drive to help is too strong to pretend otherwise. "What are you both saying?"

"We'll miss you dearly, but if you wish to return, you have our blessing."

I bounce from my seat and wrap them both in a hug, unable to contain my excitement. "Thank you! Oh, thank you so much. I will do my best to stay as safe as possible. I promise!"

Plans are already forming in my head regarding what I need to pack and do before leaving. I never thought I'd be so happy to return to such a vile place.

"There's just one thing," Dad says. "We need you to deliver a message to Chadwick."

"Why Chadwick? Can't I give it to Zade?"

"I thought you'd be happy to have a reason to talk to him."

I shrug. Interactions with Chadwick are hard enough as it is. What's more, I plain just don't want to interact with him if I don't have to.

"The fact is, Zade is already overworked." Stress lines Dad's face. How hard is this on him, having Zade, and soon me again, in Chardonia? "Chadwick can do as much, or even more than Zade in some cases, since he's not in the spotlight."

A message to Chadwick it is. I just don't know how I feel about it.

* * *

As I'm frantically throwing things into my pack, I'm making a mental note of what I'll need. I can't take much since I have to carry it all, but I should be able to pack the basics. If only the Grand Chancellor hadn't closed the borders, this would be so much easier.

"Going somewhere?"

I whirl around to see Tawny standing in my doorway, hands behind her back.

"As a matter of fact, I am. I'm going back to Chardonia." I grab an extra pair of shoes and throw them in my pack. "And don't try to talk me out of it like everyone else has done. Zade's already sent three notes telling me not to go, even though he knows better than anyone how desperately I'm needed." No word from Chadwick, though. I'll have to talk to him at some point.

"I'm not going to talk you out of it."

"Good."

"I'm going to try and talk you into taking me with you." She pulls a pack out from behind her back.

My frantic movements come to a screeching halt.

"You can stop looking like I've grown an extra head," she says.

That knocks me back into reality. "I don't know. It sort of feels like you have."

She snorts. "Mom and Dad thought so too."

"They know and are fine with you coming?"

"I wouldn't say fine."

I snap my fingers. "Under no circumstances will you be coming with me without their permission. Even with their permission, I can't imagine having to take care of you. You're one of the heirs to the throne."

"Oh, I have their permission. They just aren't fine with it."

"Well, that makes me feel better." Not.

"Please let me do this, Waverly. I need to do more than just sitting through yet another useless meeting. I need to make a difference, too."

I should probably try harder to dissuade her. Chardonia isn't a place to go on tour, especially not for an heir to the throne. But there's a glint of determination in her eyes. I doubt I could stop her even if I tried. She'd find another way to go, and it wouldn't be with someone who knows what it's like. Besides, if the Queen has given her permission, who am I to argue?

"A two-headed person may be just what I need for this trip," I say, happy to have a friend along.

"Does that mean I can join you?"

"It does."

Zade is going to kill me. Serena just might do the same.

CHAPTER 3

"I understand now why we couldn't bring our trunks." Tawny is almost out of breath from our journey up the mountainside. Though in all fairness, she's done a fantastic job so far. How does a princess stay in such good shape? From exercising more than I, a non-princess.

"Hard to decide what to bring when you have limited space, though." I scan the area until I see the rock with an 'S' etched into it. "It's just over here."

"Thank the Queen."

"You thank your own mother?"

She shrugs. "People's words rub off on me."

I stop near the entrance. "You have to promise never to reveal the location of the secret entrance into Chardonia."

"Of course not. I'm very good at keeping secrets." I suppose an heir to a country would have to be. "I'll even do the promise spell."

It's not really necessary. I do trust her, but if she's offering, I'm taking.

"All right then," I say. I think of a tie, binding us together in this secret, both a physical tie and a mental one. A bond that will keep the secret safe between the two of us. I let the spell out in a soft pink. She reaches out, and we shake hands, the pink spell encompassing our touch. Once complete, I pull my magic back in.

"Thank you. It's just that we can't be too cautious. There's only a few ways to get in Chardonia now, especially since we're not technically allowed in. We have to keep them well guarded."

"That's as it should be."

I move back around the tree and into the cave. It's dark and narrow, looking as if it ends before it even begins, but I press on, slipping through a crack in the back just wide enough for a person. It's even darker back here. I pull my energy to my core and release it in the form of pure light. Only it's not very pure. My nerves have brushed hints of green into it.

Tawny casts her own spell, white and pure with the tiniest touch of purple. I have no clue what purple means to her. Even after knowing each other our entire lives, I have a hard time reading her emotions.

As we walk through the rocky tunnel, we chat, our voices echoing through the chambers. The chamber is damp and smells of earth.

"Will they be suspicious of us being in Chardonia?"

"They are suspicious no matter if we try to enter legally or not," I reply. "If that bothers you, it'd probably be best to turn around and go home."

"I'm used to suspicion. After all, I have lived at court all my life."

"At least you've had practice. Though that's going to be one of the smaller problems."

"What's the biggest?"

"I don't know which threat is bigger yet. The council or Zade."

"Zade's temper is something fierce," Tawny replies.

"It's only gotten worse." The tunnel grows steeper, making my legs ache with exertion.

"Worse? How's that even possible?"

It's then I realize how bad it is that I haven't told her yet. The ground levels out, and we come to a cavern the size of a small room. I motion to the cave floor. "We might as well rest here."

She doesn't hesitate to follow my direction, which bodes well for how seriously she's taking this. Besides, we haven't eaten since we left and that was hours and hours ago. I'm starving, even if my nerves are trying to say otherwise.

Once we're sitting, I pull out hard tack, and we munch on it while I think on how to tell her that my brother was serious about not marrying a princess. About wanting instead another girl who's sweet and kind. A girl who barely knows magic, though I know that's not why they fell in love.

After we've been eating a few minutes, she asks, "Do I get to know how Zade's temper could have possibly gotten worse?"

I set my food down, guilt making it too difficult to eat, even if I'll need the strength later. "The girl he owned, the one he set free..."

"Serena."

The fact she remembers Serena's name is either really good or really bad. "Uh, yes, her. She um..."

"Found a way to make his temper worse?" Her expression is so neutral in the light of our wavering magic, I can't decide how she's taking this all.

"Actually, yes."

"Truly? How did she manage that?"

I just have to spit the words out, no matter how much they stick to my throat. "She captured his heart."

"Oh." The defeated word echoes through the cave.

I'm the inconsiderate person for not telling her sooner. My words grow quieter as I continue. "He proposed, and she has accepted. They are engaged to be married."

"Oh."

Guilt presses in on me more than the walls of the cave. "I'm sorry I didn't tell you sooner. I didn't know how." I'm selfish like that. And still slightly upset that I wasn't there for the engagement. Or rather, majorly upset.

Her expression remains carefully guarded. There's no telling what she's thinking. Being at court has probably given her ample opportunities to practice because she's terribly good at it. Even her spelled light hanging just above her head and to the right doesn't change color to hint at what she's feeling.

"Tawny, are you all right? Do you want to return to Envado?"

Finally, she squeezes her eyes shut as if in pain, but it's the only indication she's feeling anything. One that passes all too quickly. "I'm fine. It's just unexpected is all. He made it clear that our relationship would be no more. I was fine with that. Our parents had more plans for us than I think we did. They're still disappointed he cut it off, though they understood why when they heard of his gaining ownership of a Chardonian woman. We heard of Zade breaking the first engagement with Serena, and we thought maybe... But it's fine."

That may be what her words say, but her heart said differently when they were first engaged. "You don't have to go through with this. I can make it on my own, and Envado still needs you."

"Envado has what it needs." The skin around her eyes tightens. "I'm coming."

And so she is.

I should have told her sooner. The thought haunts me all through the tunnel, the cavern we stay the night in, and the tunnel out to Chardonian territory. I don't know if the guilt will ever leave or lessen. Sometimes I just make bad judgments. The thought still plagues me as we step into Chardonian sunlight.

The land is more beautiful than the evil hearts ruling the country. Hills covered with forest as far as the eye can see. Most women don't even know how pristine their country is because they're too busy spending their lives locked up. If Tawny wasn't present, I think I might just curse.

"This is Chardonia?" she asks, surprise tinting her words.

I glance over the forest. Rightness hums through me. This is where I belong. Where I need to be. "This is Chardonia. A place of repressed dreams and trodden hopes. Dreams and hopes we will help set free."

"I like the sound of that."

I do too. Except the problem will take more than just saying a few words to be fixed. I don't even know where to begin with helping them put the idea forward except by continuing with what I was doing before. Helping Serena with whatever she needed while trying to place hints she was worth more than she thought. It wasn't enough, but at least it was something.

A few Chardonians may have come to accept some women have the same rights as a man does, like owning themselves and land, and that women can do magic, yet there's a long, long way for them to go. The women need freedom from men. A say in things. A right to do what they want. And if most of those in power had it their way, the little progress we've made would be stomped on. The Grand Chancellor will use any means necessary to do the stomping.

CHAPTER 4

"W hat's this place?" Tawny asks.

"It's a house owned by a Chardonian who helps our cause. My friend is here also."

My skin tingles as I hurry toward the building. Suddenly, someone grips my arm and yanks me to the side. I whip my hand out, slamming it toward the side, just stopping myself from spelling Cynthia.

"You scared me." I embrace her tightly with a laugh. "It's been too long. How are you?"

"Shh." She pulls me further into the trees, Tawny following. "This house has been compromised."

"What?" I whisper, but roughly. "How did this happen?"

"I don't know. We think there's a mole."

A mole? My heart twists. Who would do this to us? Why would they do this? Everyone who's helped us acted so genuine.

She flashes a message spell that darts away. "I tried to get word to you but didn't know where you were. Lukas will meet us somewhere safer."

Not safe, but safer. Too bad I have Envadi royalty with me.

What was I thinking, letting her join me? We follow Cynthia through the trees until we reach a clearing that can be seen from the house. She stares at it, biting her lip.

I almost ask how bad it is but clamp my mouth shut. If she wanted to talk, she would have said something. Seemingly satisfied with whatever she's staring at, she motions for us to run. We take off.

Once we get going, I see what is making her so stressed. Law officers. And they're coming this way. I move faster, only in my haste, I run into a bush. Drat!

"This way," I hear one of the warlocks behind us call.

Land sakes! How are we going to ever get out of this? We're going to end up captured. My chest burns with more than the need for air as we run.

I glance back. The warlocks are closer now. I duck my head, not that it helps hide my tall height, and place myself behind Tawny.

"What are you doing?" she demands.

"Keeping you safe." I throw a spell behind me, black and thick. A blinding spell. If they can't see us, they can't hit us.

My heart pounds as we make headway. When I peek back, one of the law officers is in sight, and another comes into view, the black spell hovering behind them like a fog. They're further away than they were but still not far enough.

A golden spell flies from the closest one, straight at me and Tawny. I jump on Tawny's back, throwing us both to the ground. The spell soars over our heads, and crashes into a tree beyond us, making the inner layer visible. That could have been Tawny or me. I shiver.

But there isn't time to do more than that. I'm pulling Tawny to her feet as Cynthia bursts an emerald spell at them. They slow as it hits, coughing.

We press harder, running until my already sore legs burn.

Cynthia turns and aims a burgundy spell at our pursuers. It slows them enough that they are out of sight, but they zap several spells our direction. Cynthia throws a dark red shield spell up, protecting all three of us from the attack.

As we continue to run, I can't help but wonder what I've done by bringing Tawny into Chardonia. This isn't the welcome I wanted for her or me.

"Get back here, wenches," one of them calls.

Yeah, like that'll entice us to stop.

Tawny flashes a pink spell behind us. It goes out of sight for a moment, only to flare up.

"Got them," she says.

I gasp for breath as we continue to pull ahead. Cynthia covers our tracks with a spell I don't take time to study, though I'd love to see how she does this one. My own track-covering spell isn't what it should be.

After we've been running off and on for what seems like all day but is probably closer to an hour, Cynthia stops us. She looks around and then moves a dead bush to reveal a cave entrance. Despite how hard the cave floor is, we all collapse on it, heaving for breath.

"That was not fun," I say.

Tawny nods. Oh lands, her parents will never trust me again when they learn how serious of a situation I've dragged their daughter into. Why did they ever agree to let her come? They know things are unstable here and getting worse.

Suddenly, Lukas is hugging Cynthia, gripping her tightly and whispering in her ear. I stare the other way, trying hard not to intrude on their moment.

"Are you two well?" he asks us after finally letting Cynthia out of the hug but still keeping an arm around her.

I wait for Tawny to nod before saying, "We're fine. What happened?"

"I don't know," Cynthia says. "Things seemed to be going well and were safe, but this morning while Lukas and I were on our way back from a walk, we saw several law officers go in the house. We hid in the trees but never saw them come out. And…"

"There was screaming," Lukas finishes for her, his voice hushed.

Pain shoots through me. "But George has been working with us for years."

"They are determined to have me," Cynthia says. "I showed everyone what women can do with magic, and they want to annihilate that."

Determination fills me. "They can try, but they won't succeed."

"No, they won't. There have been a few other girls who have run away from home. I'm going to try and find them."

"That sounds like a good plan. Do you need help?" I ask, excited there is a chance for me to do something.

"I think it'd be best if Lukas and I keep the search group small."

"I should really move on anyway." Though I long for a way to do more.

"Go to Serena," Cynthia says.

"Thank you."

If only Serena's family situation weren't so fragile. If only her stupid father wasn't around so I could go directly to the girls. Better yet, if only I could spell his lights out. "I just don't know if we can get there safely now without the male chaperone our contact was supposed to provide."

"I can take you and catch up with Cynthia later," Lukas says.

"Haven't they been coming down on foreigners?"

"Yes, but we're not completely banned. It will be less hassle for me to be caught than you."

"He's right," Cynthia says, though I can tell it makes her nervous by the way she twists her hands together. "Take him with you. Please give my love to Serena." Her voice aches with longing.

"Of course I will." I give her a tight hug. "I hope to see you soon."

She hugs Lukas. "Come back to me."

"You know I will," he replies.

They kiss, fierce and loving. I turn away to give them privacy. At least someone understands what love is.

CHAPTER 5

Looking at the house Serena's staying in, I'm grateful for the choice to come here instead of Zade's, even if it meant taking longer to get here. Lukas got us here safely, so hopefully he can return the same way. And now I'm not only where I need to be, but I don't have to face Zade's wrath quite yet. Unless he's visiting Serena.

I gulp past the thought, even though it's highly likely, especially the way things have been going since our arrival. When Zade and Chadwick find out I'm not only here, but I've brought Tawny with me, there will be two very angry warlocks.

At least, I assume there'll be two. Perhaps it will be only my brother and not the man everyone expects me to marry. It's been so long since I've heard from Chadwick. Maybe he doesn't care where I am. Maybe he's so wrapped up in the reason he left Envado in the first place to help the Chardonian people that I'm only a distant memory. I don't know if the thought is for better or worse. Whichever it is, I have to find him and deliver the message from my father in person.

They'll soon know we're here, if they don't already. Warlocks are visibly guarding the house, not even trying to hide like when I left. Have things gotten worse here as well?

"Let's go see Serena."

Tawny follows me and Lukas up the walkway. "Does she know I'm coming?"

More trouble. "I told her someone was joining me."

"But she doesn't know who I am."

"I told her your name," I hedge.

She gives me a look. "But not who I am."

"Fine. I didn't tell her of your previous relationship with Zade." I eye Lukas, knowing I can trust him, but it's probably best to keep her identity from being spread around even with those we trust. "Or anything else."

Her entire posture takes on a regal bearing. "She needs to know. About me and Zade at least."

At least she agrees about keeping her royalty status under wraps, even if it's clear just by the way she acts. "I know. Only there are more pressing things happening than just relationships." And it makes me feel like the worst friend for keeping their former engagement a secret. Why am I doing this?

"True. It's not as if I'm here to steal Zade."

Lukas gives her a sharp look. She'd better not be. As much as she's a friend to me, and possibly even my future queen, I won't let anyone put Serena through more grief.

Before I can reply, the door bursts open, and Serena's coming to me with a big grin on her face. "I can't believe you're here! I didn't know if I would ever see you again."

"It was only a little over a week." But I hug her tight anyway like it's been years.

"Let's get inside," she says when I let her go, eying Tawny.

She ushers the three of us in quickly, looking around as if there's something to fear. If I hadn't already known things were getting worse, this would confirm it. When she closes the door behind us and bolts it, her entire body eases.

"How about I make you a treat?" I say.

"You just got here. You don't need to cook anything," Serena says as she leads us through the house.

"Hasn't it been too long since you had cinnamon cookies?"

She laughs. "You know my weakness, but if you want time to settle in first, it's fine."

"I can settle later. Food is much more important." Always more important than dealing with necessary chores.

She leads us to the kitchen, which is smaller than Zade's or even the house that's now her father's again, but it's workable. I don't hesitate to get cooking, looking through cupboards and pulling things out.

"How are your mother and the girls?"

"Who's this you brought with you?" Serena asks, ignoring my question.

It must be really bad for them. Maybe I don't want to know how bad until there's something I can do about it. Still, I will try to find out when she seems more open to talking.

Tawny is graciously waiting next to a wall, looking so regal I expect any moment to have one of them shout that I've brought royalty with me because I'm a dunce. And an even bigger dunce for not giving introductions right away. Even if I'm not going to reveal exactly who her parents are, she deserves my respect both because of who she is to my country and as my friend.

"Sorry, the excitement of the moment caught up with me. This is Tawny, a very good friend of mine."

"I'm happy to have met you, Tawny," Serena says. "Even if the circumstances are not what I'd have them be."

"Thank you."

"Come sit by me while Waverly makes us something mouth-watering." When Serena sits down at the counter to watch me, the time and strain is immediately evident by the lines of worry etched in her face. Tawny eases into the chair next to her, back rigid. I suppose even court doesn't prepare one for sitting next to your ex-fiancée's new fiancée.

"How are the girls, really?" I ask Serena about her sisters.

Her shoulders seem to cave into the rest of her. "I've only managed to sneak in to see them once. The girls aren't handling things well. Most of them seem to be shutting down. Bethany's doing what she can for them, but I'm afraid of the strain it's causing her. Especially as she tries to take care of Mother."

"Will the baby be born soon?"

"Within the next month or two. She seems to be taking this pregnancy harder than the others. Don't tell her I said this, but I think she's getting too old for this. I wish there was a way to rescue all of them before then. It's going to be very unpleasant when she has another girl."

Unpleasant to say the least. Who knows how Stephen will take his wrath out on his wife and daughters? I wish I could march over there right now and slam a hex into him so hard he wouldn't wake for a year. Never mind that I lack the power to actually do so.

Serena opens her mouth but closes it again before saying, "Zade said you weren't coming. I didn't tell him about the letter you sent claiming the opposite."

"Don't know if he'll like the fact you're keeping secrets from him."

"You can't keep a secret from someone who isn't around to speak with."

Lands, Zade, how are you treating your intended this time? Sometimes my brother needs a hit over the head with a frying pan to knock some sense into him. "Well, what he doesn't know will keep things going smoothly enough."

"That will change as soon as he knows you're here and can get away from his duties," Serena continues. "He's not going to be happy."

"So all his letters told me." Over and over again. "You didn't really think I'd stay away, did you?"

"No, but part of me hoped you would."

A slice of pain cuts through me. "You don't want me here?"

"I only said a part. It's just that as much as we love your company, I fear for your safety."

"As Zade fears for yours."

"Yes, but there was a reason Zade sent you away. Things are changing. Things I can help with, and I need to do what I can for my sisters and Mother. But if I had left with you, or if I went now, who would take my place? Who will do what they can to protect my sisters? Who will show Chardonian women what sort of life they can have? What sort of power they can have? What sort of freedom they can have from being owned?"

"That's exactly why we're here as well."

"But it doesn't have to be your fight. You're not a Chardonian."

I stand taller. "Just by being a person in this world, it's my fight."

Serena gives the faintest of smiles before turning to Tawny. "What do you think? Did you come for the same reason? Did she warn you how dangerous things are?"

The mention of danger makes me wonder if she knows about Cynthia's situation, but I don't want to place more worries on her if she hasn't heard Cynthia has dealt with it as needed, and the Sanos contacts have been notified. There's nothing Serena could do about it but worry more.

Tawny says, "I was warned, but I need to be here. I'm sick of leading an idle life that is useless to anyone."

"You've found a precarious way to try, but if Waverly brought you I won't turn you away. Do you know magic?"

This is such a good change from having Serena cringe away from even the faintest hint of magic.

When Tawny doesn't reply, I say, "She's much better at it than I." Magic tutors are required for the next monarch. Those protection spells she was required to learn are stronger than an entire mountain.

"You're much too kind." Tawny blushes.

"Good," Serena says. "Even if Waverly is exaggerating, we could use the help. I'm trying to learn and am coming across more and more women who are requesting help to learn as well."

She was warming up to it when I left, but I didn't expect her to willingly get so involved. Things really are changing. With Serena at least.

CHAPTER 6

The door slams. Serena jumps, but I know that sound all too well. Zade is here.

I take a deep breath and prepare myself for battle. Tawny is resting in our shared room, which I should have been doing as well, but sleep wouldn't come. Instead, I sought Serena out to find more details about what's been going on. I should have forced myself to stay in bed, though it'd be cruel to leave Serena alone with his wrath. At least she can probably calm him better than I can.

Zade storms in with a force of tense muscles and a glare in his eyes that could turn into magic sparks at any moment. Serena relaxes back into her chair with a giant grin on her face. Either she doesn't realize how seriously his temper is flaming right now, or she doesn't care.

"What are you doing here?" His words boom at me.

It's then I realize Chadwick is behind him. I stare at him, ignoring Zade's fuming. My heart doesn't give a thump or a flutter or anything at all. Why can't it respond to him like I think it should? Like everyone expects it to? Maybe my idea of how loves feels, how it looks from outside, is wrong. Maybe the warmth of friendship is all there is for someone like me.

"Waverly!"

I roll my eyes and say in my sweetest voice, "Yes, Master Zade?"

"Don't you dare give me that. This isn't the time for jokes. Mom and Dad are going to have a heart attack when they realize you didn't listen to me and returned. You should know your brother only wants to keep you safe. What's that going to do to Dad? Did you think of him when you went gallivanting off?"

He's right. It's not the time for games even if it's fun to tweak him. There are some things too precious to joke over. "They're the ones who told me to come."

This seems to trip him up. He pinches the bridge of his nose. "Why would they do that?"

"Because they understand as much as I do that I need to be here."

He huffs. Serena goes to him and puts a hand on his arm. The change is instant. His eyes soften, and his shoulders relax. He kisses her full on the mouth like none of us are even there. I glance away, which leads to catching Chadwick's eye. I hurry to stare at my hands. More awkward than when I accidentally spelled his hair pink.

I make an exaggerated sound of clearing my throat.

Zade gives an exasperated sigh. "Well, you're clearly not in the mood for my temper, so just let me and my fiancée have some time together. Maybe then, just maybe, I'll be able to talk to you without wanting to strangle you."

"By all means, go right ahead. It sounds as if you've been neglecting her."

He growls. "Stupid council."

"Oh, just kiss me again," Serena says.

I turn away as he passionately does so. I'm all for true love and kissing, but my brother doesn't seem like the best person to illustrate the point. Ew.

Chadwick hurries past the couple, turning away from them as soon as he can. The kissing must bother him too. Or maybe it's my presence that's causing issues. At least Serena and Zade finally seem to take a hint and move into the hall.

Chadwick takes the chair Serena vacated. "You shouldn't have come back."

"I think my brother already made that clear enough."

"We have seven warlocks guarding this house every day. There's a lot of people who come here to learn more about what Serena's done and to hear more about Cynthia. About what they're doing with freedom and magic. But some guests aren't as harmless as they appear. Attacks are almost a daily occurrence. And..."

Almost daily? I knew it was bad but not this bad. "And what?"

"It's not just that I'm trying to keep you safe because I care about you. It's..."

My chest gives a strange little twist. The warmth of friendship could be enough. But I doubt it would spark kisses the likes of which came from Zade and Serena. Besides, doesn't he deserve that as well? "And what, Chadwick?"

"And I don't think having a Chardonian, especially a female Chardonian, in the house will help."

"Zade and you are already here, what difference does it make?"

"Zade is at least on the council, and no one notices me when he's around. I'm just a shadow," he says. "Things are bad enough without adding to it."

This is exactly what I didn't want to hear. Of course I knew they sent me away for a reason, but I thought it was just for my own safety. How can I endanger Serena more? Some people still think we're cruel giants, barbarians, not worth being near.

In any case, he needs his message. "Dad sent me to tell you something." I scoot closer. Even in this house that is supposed to be safe, rebellion words aren't to be treated lightly. Exactly why Dad didn't just send a spell message. "The Envadi rebels are lessening. With the borders closed, not only is it harder for them to get in, but they don't want to come in. We're on our own with whatever is already set up here."

"That's the note your dad sent? Why in all of Envado did he send you here if he knew things were getting worse?" He jumps to his feet.

Tawny picks just that moment to enter, a big, silly grin on her face that falters the moment she glances into the hall. Zade and Serena must not have gone far.

"Tawny!" Chadwick practically shouts.

Instantly, there's a giant thump from the hall, and Zade appears. Serena is not far behind with eyebrows crinkled. I am in so much trouble.

"What are you doing here?" Zade demands Tawny.

Well, there's the fact that this is not only very awkward but also unexpected. He'll probably chew me out for bringing her as well, but I wasn't going to be the one to stop her.

She glances at the floor, back rigid. She could give these perfect posture Chardonian girls competition. "I wanted to help like Waverly."

Zade is still staring at her. More like gaping.

"Of course you already know each other," Serena says, not realizing what she's walking into. What I didn't get around to warning her about. "I should have realized if you knew Waverly, you'd know Chadwick and Zade."

That's such a small portion of it.

Tawny looks away from us all. Zade seems like he's going to rip his nose right off with how hard he's rubbing it.

"We're all acquainted," I say.

Zade glares at me. "You are either completely inane or mad."

"She's both," Chadwick says.

"Hey, I—" deserve both of their comments entirely. "Her parents agreed, and it was her idea to begin with."

"You could have said no," Zade snaps. "They should have said no."

"And you could all talk with me instead of around me," Tawny snaps.

We all scuff our boots on the floor.

Serena glances at Tawny, clearly confused. "Is there a reason your coming is worse than Waverly being here? This all seems a little extreme and everyone seems to know why except me."

Tawny seems to remember herself then. "They just don't think I can protect myself properly." Her voice lowers. "And..." She eyes Zade.

"And she's my previous fiancée," he admits.

"Oh." Serena's face goes calm. Too calm. "Well then, can I get you something to drink and eat? You didn't eat much earlier."

"That would be lovely, thank you." Tawny's training has probably never been tried so thoroughly.

Zade mumbles some claim about needing to check on the guards, and Chadwick hurries out after him. Neither Serena nor Tawny respond but avoid eye contact as the men walk outside. What a fine place to leave us in. And I don't know which of us has it worse. Tawny intruding on Zade's new love, Serena just meeting his old fiancée, or me for being the biggest dunce for bringing them all together.

CHAPTER 7

The day doesn't get any more comfortable after that, but at least everyone pretends it is. When I get Serena alone and ask her about it, she claims it's fine. She still has trouble opening up to others, even if we've known each other over a year now. Tawny won't say anything either, but at least she doesn't pretend there's not a problem, just that she doesn't wish to discuss it.

I toss and turn all night, unable to sleep for thoughts of our situation. I don't just worry about bringing Tawny here but also Chadwick saying our presence will make it worse for Serena. Which also means worse for Tawny. Even though it's dangerous here, I need to keep her in a place that's safe, if such a thing is possible in a place like Chardonia. At the same time, not clue her into the fact I'm keeping her safe because she'd be livid to know she can help, but I'm not letting her.

I find Serena in the barn brushing Goldie. She pats the horse down, speaking in a soothing voice. Does it do more good for her or the horse? It's difficult to say.

"Morning," I greet her.

"I thought you'd be making breakfast."

"Who, me?" I tease. "It's good that Zade was able to sneak

Goldie away before Stephen got a hold of her." Her dad is the biggest jerk of them all.

She nods, though her expression remains passive. "I just wish I could ride her more. But it's too dangerous for me to go gallivanting out in the open."

"That must be hard." When she doesn't say anything, I decide I just need to come out with it. "There's something we need to discuss."

She starts flicking the brush rougher. "I already told you I don't wish to speak about it."

"Not about yesterday, about something else," I say. "Tawny and I have been talking."

At the mention of Tawny, Serena goes oddly still. Despite saying she doesn't want to talk about it, she doesn't stop me.

"We think we should find work in another household." The explanation doesn't have to do with her being in more danger because of our presence, but it has to be the right choice. She'd likely insist her safety isn't jeopardized by me even if it is. "Tawny wants to see more of Chardonia, and I think I'd like to go with her. Maybe somewhere where they aren't as antagonistic toward us Envadi, but where we can still do some good."

And keep everyone safe.

"You're going to leave us? You just arrived." Her big eyes are so sad, it makes me wish things were different. Safer.

"I want to stay. I missed you so much. More than I would have ever thought. But I came back to help. I feel like you have the help you need here now, and there may be something more I can do elsewhere."

"I understand." She's silent a moment but continues brushing Goldie. "I may have somewhere that fits your needs. Councilman Daniel and Annabelle are very opened-minded, but there are other servants in their household and people they visit with that you may be able to reach out to."

"I remember them. They'd be perfect if they're willing." I give her a tight hug. "Thank you. Would you mind giving us a reference?"

"I doubt you'll need it, but I'd be delighted to help both you and Tawny."

"Thank you for your help," I say. "Do you also think maybe it will help you by not having her around?"

For a moment, I think she's going to disagree, but then she says, "I admit, the thought crossed my mind. I'm certain we'd be fine if she stayed, though, and I will miss you."

"I will miss you too." I wrap her in a hug, tightly like she was my own sister. "I better go help with breakfast."

"I knew it."

"You already know me too well." I turn to leave.

"Waverly?"

"Yes?"

"Is your leaving because of Tawny being Zade's previous fiancée?"

I swallow past the tightness in my throat. "Zade loves you. He would never, ever leave you for anyone else. I've never seen a love as fierce as his."

"Yet, you're going."

"It will be good for us. All of us."

I'm not sure she entirely believes my response, and she shouldn't, just not for the reasons she supposes.

CHAPTER 8

Leaving Serena again is harder than I expect. Even harder than being so close to Serena's sisters and not being able to see them. There's an ache inside me without them here. Serena promises to send word if there's any news or change with them and when her mother has the baby.

Tawny is silent the entire ride except for once saying, "I always thought the windowless carriages were an exaggeration. If anything I see now that it was under exaggerated."

I've never seen Annabelle and Councilman Daniel's house before. It's large, though not as grand as Zade's. Ivy climbs up one side of their house, over all three floors reaching the roof. The rest of their house is white, with a good number of windows.

Annabelle greets us with a smile, wearing a pair of tan breeches. No one has embraced Katherine's designs as much as she has. Not only is Katherine, a friend who pretends to be a tarnished, an amazing seamstress, but she has a flair for women's independence that influences others. Knowing Annabelle gets along so well with her makes me feel more at home already. "I'm so glad you've decided to join us. When Serena told me not one, but two Envadi were looking for a place to work, I was delighted. Let's have a sip of tea and discuss your duties."

As we move to the sitting room, Tawny asks, "Do you typically take tea with the servants?"

She most definitely does not sound like a servant herself. It will be a miracle if she can not only do her work but do it without giving away who she really is.

"Usually, and of course, since Waverly and I have met, I couldn't pass up an opportunity to get to know another Envadi." She insists on pouring the tea for us both, and once we're all settled, she leans in close and whispers. "Do either of you use magic?"

I want to exchange a glance with Tawny to know what she thinks of this, but I don't dare give us away so blatantly. Instead, I mimic Annabelle by leaning closer and whispering, "Do you?"

She giggles like my evasive reply pleased her and, with a wink, pours more tea in my cup. "I think we shall all get along just fine."

We chatter as we sip our tea. Annabelle and Tawny agree to try her as Annabelle's personal maid while I'll help with general housework. It suits me and keeps Tawny more with someone I trust and myself out moving among the other servants. Hopefully, since Annabelle and Daniel have accepted me, we'll get rid of their notions that I'm a barbarian, and what's more, convince them of women's worth.

Once we're finished, Annabelle instructs another servant to show us around, including where we'll be working, our bed chamber, where we are to report each morning, and where to eat.

The servant is nice, but quick, hurrying through the house as if it's a struggle just to find a little time to show us around, even though doing so will mean we'll be able to help ease her load. The last place she takes us is a tiny room.

"These are the living quarters you'll be sharing. The Councilman was kind enough to install a flushing toilet down the hall we all share. We may even get the electric lights in our quarters if things continue to go well."

It would be a nicer prospect if it wasn't already expected. It's hard to remember people live without these things and think it's perfectly normal. Electricity and flushing toilets should be as standard as food. Especially the toilets.

"That sounds wonderful." I fake a smile.

"We're excited you're both joining us," she replies.

"Thank you," Tawny speaks up for the first time since we left Annabelle. Her good manners never fail, even when she most likely feels like keeping silent.

"You can unpack and come help in the kitchen when you're finished if you'd like. It'd give you both a chance to get to know the others."

"We'll be there shortly." Once she's gone, I ask Tawny, "What do you think so far?"

"She was nice."

"Hopefully, the others are as well."

"Annabelle is great at the very least. She's the one I'll be spending most of my time with anyway."

"Remember to be really careful about how you do magic. Some women are aware they can do it, but that doesn't mean the council will let them."

"Of course."

Will the strides we're trying to make with these people ever be enough?

* * *

I'M SO FOCUSED on Tawny and how she's taking everything and if she's giving anything away about who she is or the magic she can do. If only I had her skills when I was here, maybe I could have taught Cynthia something more useful. It doesn't matter. It's too late. Cynthia survived and won the tournament, even if she's now on the run. Thousands of Chardonians know about her and what she did, too many minds for the council to erase.

Mine feels erased. After all my wool gathering, all the servants are heading off to their duties. One of the other servant girls shows me my duties for the day and leaves me to clean the study while she goes off to accomplish her own chores.

I start with dusting the bookshelves, wishing I could pick up one of the books to read instead of cleaning them. Being Serena's maid was a lot more exciting than cleaning all the time. At least I usually had someone to chat with. I trace my finger down the spine of one of the books. It's unfamiliar, but the title is interesting. My fingers itch to pick it up and see if there's something good inside.

"What are you doing?" A harsh male voice demands.

I whirl around, my feather duster landing right on a warlock's chin.

He coughs and smacks it away. "You're supposed to be cleaning the room, not covering me in dirt."

"I didn't know you were standing so close." Not much of an apology but true.

"Excuse me? Did you just make an excuse instead of doing your job?" Now that he's smacking the dirt off his face, it easier to see his firm jaw line, golden brown eyes, and dark hair.

"Just letting you know why it happened. I don't usually greet strangers in such fashion."

He wipes his face with a handkerchief before yanking the duster out of my hand. "Neither do I, but for you I'll make an exception since you haven't learned Chardonian ways. Do not address me so informally again. I may be a servant, but I'm still a warlock. You will treat me with the respect I deserve. Call me sir or Master Jack."

Is he serious? This whiner deserves absolutely no respect.

"While you manage to stay in this position," the tone of his voice implies it won't be for long, but Annabelle will surely keep us here as long as we'd like, "you will defer to me in all things."

"All things?" Just who does he think he is?

"Are you daft? That's what I just stated."

I shouldn't. Oh, I know I shouldn't. But I just can't help it. "Even picking out which stockings I'm going to wear for the day?"

For the briefest moment his face transforms, almost like he's about to smile, but before I've had time to decide if he really did, his face is an inch from mine, eyes narrowed. "Do not play games with me, girl."

The playful spark catches fire, heat flaming my words. "I'm no girl, unless you're just a boy since we must be about the same age. Of course, the way you're throwing a tantrum, it must be you never grew out of being a spoiled toddler."

His mouth tightens into a firm, condemning line. "I won't hesitate hexing you if you step out of line."

Though he doesn't move, it feels as if his weight is pressing into me, forcing me to back off. I refuse to budge, staring him down. Would Annabelle and the Councilman allow him such liberties? I doubt they'd be happy about it, but I've often been surprised in this country. No matter. It's a known fact now that women do magic. If he tries anything, he's going to get a surprise blasted back in his face that will have him ruing the day he ever looked my way.

Finally, he eases from my space, slowly though, like he wants his threat to linger long after he's gone. There's a threat that will linger all right. The threat of me hexing his hair purple and his nose and ear hair to grow to his shoulders.

When he's several feet from me, I feel like I can breathe again. Only the air isn't cool enough to douse my anger.

"Return to your work. When you're finished, go scrub the toilets and remember your place." He strides toward the door.

"You're only a servant, too. Like you have room to talk about remembering my place."

He swings toward me, eyes wild, and my magic pounds through me. "I am a Chardonian warlock. I may be working to keep my family out of debt, but I am nothing, *nothing*, like you."

Before I can give another flip response, he stomps off. My magic still pounds through me like boulders falling from a cliff. What a jerk.

"And keep your hands off those books," he yells over his shoulder. "Chardonian women only read the Woman's Canon. While you're here, you will do the same."

Double jerk.

He stalks from the room, leaving clouds of anger in his wake. I don't know whose are bigger, mine or his.

As soon as he's gone, I let a firework spell fly, having enough presence of mind to keep it the size of an apple. If only I could direct it at him. Zade isn't the only one in our family with a temper. It's only unfortunate I kept a tight lid on it instead of fully letting it out to teach that jerk how women really can behave. Stuck in the middle of a temper tantrum is enough to get me in trouble. Though I suppose hitting him with the spell would have been worse. That would have been a fantastic report for my first day of work.

I return to dusting, walking around like all the books are fake and don't need special treatment anyway. It doesn't last long. Even if that brute can't treat me with the respect I deserve, I can treat these books better. I'll just have to pretend they're all about math so I'm not tempted to open them again.

It's not until several minutes later when I've almost finished the room, I realize he threatened to hex me. But even though he seemed past ready to do so, he didn't. Most Chardonian men have no such problem. A woman looking at them is enough of an excuse to hex them, especially ones so clearly rooted in their own superiority. I stare out the now empty doorway. So why didn't he hex me?

CHAPTER 9

"How was your first day?" Tawny asks.

"How was yours?" I reply, hoping the evasive tactic works. Not only am I still confused by the incident with the brute, but I'm fuming from scrubbing toilets the rest of the day. I thought I was grateful for them yesterday, but that's been over-trodden by the plethora of toilets. Disgusting.

"Annabelle is really sweet. I like her a lot. She's going to be so much fun to work with. I always heard Chardonian women wear only dresses, but her wardrobe varies as much as the topics she likes to discuss."

"Cynthia and Annabelle are the only women in Chardonia I'm aware of that wear breeches in front of company. And Annabelle is cautious to only wear them when she's here, never in front of anyone outside of her closest friends."

"Oh. Well, if that's all she'll wear them for, I'm glad she considers me a friend."

A twinge of jealousy pulls through me, but it's not of use to anyone. I was the one who chose it to be this way. If I was not working with Tawny and Annabelle, there would be a lot fewer people I could influence. This way I have more opportunities, even if it means dealing with warlock scum like Jack. Unless of course, he keeps me scrubbing toilets all the time.

"You never answered my question. How was your first day?"

With Jack still lingering in my thoughts, it's hard to think of a decent lie. "It was a day."

"That bad?"

I puff my pillow. "I'm sure things will go smoother tomorrow."

* * *

I GATHER SHEETS and head for the laundry room. These people really need to get more appliances. Their lives would be so much simpler. At least I'm not scrubbing toilets today, though the laundry room is steaming in a way that's almost worse than cleaning toilets.

"Are those from an extra room?" Jack startles me.

I jump, dropping the sheets.

"Perfect. At least they haven't been cleaned yet." I bend down to gather them together before looking up. Sarcasm can't help but lace my words. "I'm so sorry, *sir*. These will be cleaned as soon as I pick them off the floor from where I dropped them after you scared me. And yes, they're from an extra room, the blue one."

His eyes tighten, just like they did yesterday, and I prepare myself for another lecture. And to discover how much like a typical Chardonian warlock he is. Will he attempt to hex me as I suspect he will?

"Look, about yesterday—"

"Don't bother. The last thing I need to add to this day is another one of your *helpful* chats."

"Fine. Just keep doing your job." He storms off.

Good riddance. By the time I finish gathering the sheets, guilt is nudging in. It wasn't really his fault I dropped the sheets. Sure, he could have been louder, but I could have been more graceful, or at least gracious. It almost sounded like he was going to apologize before I cut him off.

I grumble at myself all the way to the laundry room before pasting on a fake smile. No sense being rude to them as well, especially since these are the very people whose opinions I'm working on changing.

I spend a few minutes talking with the other servants in the laundry room, being warm and friendly, even though all I feel like doing is shooting a few rounds at spelled targets like those Zade is so fond of. Pushing that desire aside, the girls seem friendly enough, so I must be passably convincing.

We talk of mundane things at first, but it quickly becomes apparent that they have a higher opinion of themselves than most Chardonian women. They don't cower or lower their heads, even when a man walks in the room. Annabelle and Daniel have already done an amazing job with most of them. Maybe there is more hope for this country than I thought could happen in a short time.

After giving a merry goodbye, I scoot back into the hall, heading for the next room I'm to clean. I've gone far enough that I'm no longer in the main hall and shouldn't have anyone passing by, when I slouch against the wall.

What am I doing here?

I suppose coming to an Envadi friendly home should have been my first clue I wouldn't be needed. Maybe I can find another place where my skills will be more useful while Tawny stays here.

While I'm still slouched against the wall, Annabelle comes into view. Peeling myself up, I plaster another smile on my face before she sees me moping.

"Waverly. Just who I was looking for."

My smile feels more genuine. "Glad we could bump into each other then. What can I help you with?"

"I just wanted to say thank you for coming. Tawny is a lovely breath of fresh air. I simply adore her company."

She does have that effect on people. "She said she enjoys being with you as well."

Dimples form as Annabelle's smile grows. "Are you happy as well? If not, I could find a different position for you. Something you're more accustomed to."

Like she needs two lady's maids. Besides, my thoughts on finding another place were probably correct. I'll just stay long enough to make Serena's reference of me worthwhile and to make certain Annabelle knows I'm grateful for this opportunity.

"Thank you, I'm happy where I am."

"No problems with any of the other servants?"

Are you kidding me? I want to throw hexes at Jack every time I see him and, as a rule, I don't cast hexes. "They are all so welcoming."

"Wonderful. We try hard to have a happy staff that works together." I'll give her credit for that. Most of them are genuinely kind. "Most are working off debts, you know, and Councilman Daniel feels it's important for them to be able to do so. Yet, we also strive to have people working for us with attitudes conducive toward working together. Whether a warlock or not."

Maybe she knows what a pest Jack is already. I lie through my teeth. "They certainly are all wonderful."

"There's one other thing I wanted to mention. I've already spoken with Tawny, but since it's your first time with us, I thought it would be best if I told you directly. There's to be a council meeting here tomorrow." My ears perk up, and I work to not seem too elated over the possibility. "It would be best if you let the other servants handle everything since they are familiar with it. In truth, it would be best if you either stuck to your own room or came with Tawny and kept me company in my room. Things with Envado are so tense, I'd hate to see the council take it out on you two."

"I'll probably stick to my own room. Get a chance to rest up." Like resting is what I'm going to be doing. Guilt pricks at me for not telling her more, but I'm not about to involve her in the scheme that's forming.

"Perfectly understandable. I'm sure it'd do you some good and help give you more time to adjust. But if you change your mind, please feel free to join us."

"Might I tonight, perhaps? I would really enjoy talking with you."

"That would be lovely."

"I'll bring a glass of warm milk, then."

She laughs. "Tawny tried that last night. I fear a glass of water suits me just fine."

"What is it with Chardonians not enjoying warm milk?"

"We're smart like that."

She laughs as I make my way out of the hallway. There's much to think on now.

A council meeting. This is perfect. Even if I'm supposed to stay to my room, there's no way I'll stay locked up when the best opportunity just came my way. Perhaps I won't have to leave after all. Except I can't cause any problems for her or the Councilman. It's not only my own life at risk. Yet there must be something I can do.

CHAPTER 10

Once I've parted ways with Annabelle, I don't waste any time. I make my way, not for the room I'm supposed to clean next, but to find where they're holding the council meeting. I'll clean the other rooms during the night if I have to make up for it. Though maybe this is why they need to be cleaned? Are some of them staying overnight? Maybe I can do something with that as well, but I can't chance that on a hunch. I need something firm to grab on to. Something that will work. No questions asked.

It doesn't take long to find it. Remembering the biggest yet most secluded rooms from our tour leaves few options. Plus servants are swarming it. Which is good as a confirmation, but bad for carrying through with my plan.

Most of them are bringing in chairs, but three of them stay to clean. It's probably just as well. I'm sure the council check for spells before they start the meeting. It's a common enough practice in Envado in any case from what Tawny has told me previously.

If Zade would stop being so stubborn and tell me what's going on with the political side of things so I could better help, I wouldn't be so desperate to figure it out on my own. Though it's hard to be too upset with him since I know he's just trying to protect me. Things have gotten worse for him with more pressure from the Grand Chancellor and other warlocks since I was gone. Whatever he's doing, he's working desperately to keep the council happy while desperately trying to help the Chardonian women.

No wonder he didn't want me around to give him one more thing to worry over. Too bad. There's good I can do. I know it. Enough of just teaching girls how to spell their nails. Well, I'm not entirely done with it. Wouldn't want to go without style, but I'll work on it in addition to better spells.

With that thought to embolden me, I enter the room pretending like this is exactly where I was sent. An idea has to come to me. If not, well, it can't be any worse than scrubbing toilets and hot laundry rooms. "I'm here to help. What would you like me to do?"

One of the servants, the only male of the group says to me, "Clean the windows. And do a good job. The Grand Chancellor likes the light shining behind him as much as possible."

"Of course." Perfect. Not only does it get me in here, but it is a lot better than what I was doing before.

I help myself to the pile of cleaning supplies and get busy on the windows. Only, not too busy. I take my time scrubbing every speck I see, and not just the ones I see, but ones that aren't really there. Even though I'm going to such lengths, the others are taking just as long while keeping the talking to a minimum. He wasn't kidding about how clean the Grand Chancellor likes it.

Shining the tabletop and scrubbing the floors with such vigor, it's easy to believe they take the threat of the Grand Chancellor coming seriously.

But it hampers my time alone. So when I'm certain they're all focused on their own tasks, I swipe my hand on the edge of the glass, leaving a smudge. I purposefully avoid it while I tackle the rest of the windows.

I'm on the bottom of the last window, the last one I have to do, other than the spot I'm pretending I don't see. Thankfully, the others are finally packing up their things. I thought they'd never get there. I can still make something happen, and I think I know what.

One of the servants leaves the room, but the male servant who told me what to do asks, "Are you almost finished? The rest of us have other duties we need to attend to."

Technically, so do I. "Yes, I think I'm done." I step back and pretend to scan the window. "Oh, drat! I missed a big ol' spot."

My voice is too fake, but all the same, he shakes his head at me, like the only thing he realizes is I'm an incompetent Envadi servant. I move to the spot and take my time not just cleaning the spot, but everything around it.

"Finish up then. We can't stay to help," he says.

"That's fine. I'll manage it." I turn to see his reaction, but he and the remaining servant are already gone. Guess my job really doesn't matter to them at all.

I continue puttering around for a minute, in case they decide to return. When no one appears, I quickly swipe down the spot and dive under the table closest to the window.

After studying the room, I think this is the best place to hide a voice-activated spell so no one can see the flash when it activates. Of course, I'll have to focus on calming myself down, leaving as little emotions as possible to show when it does activate. It will be perfect. Or at least, there's nowhere else to hide it so it will have to be perfect.

I search the bottom of the table for the best nook to hide it in. The legs meet the table every foot or so, but the corners have two legs that meet together, creating more of a nook. It needs to be as small as possible, tucked back beneath other parts of the table preferably. Even then, there's a chance it may get caught and that would be bad. Very, very bad.

Poor Annabelle and Councilman Daniel would probably get in trouble for it, even if the warlocks know it's not from them. I'm certain they need to protect the meetings at their house. One more reason not to get caught. I can't bring that down on them. But if I let the opportunity go without doing something. I'd regret it too much, even if it means taking a risk. It's a risk I'll keep taking as long as I'm here. Maybe I won't need to find a new place to work after all.

Finally, I spot a small nook hidden behind one of the legs where it joins the table. Perfect. Now, to make a spell that's activated by Zade's voice. I think that will work. Maybe. It may mean missing some details if he doesn't speak right away, but hopefully it also means it goes undetected. Unless they search for spells in the middle of their meeting. There should be no need for that. I hope.

I take several, deep calming breaths, trying to clear as much emotion as I can. Only, as soon as I start to think of the spell I need to do, emotions flood through me. Memories mixed with giggling and scoldings. Zade and I used to use a spell similar to the one I'm about to cast to listen to Mom and Dad talk. We always wanted to find out what sort of presents and surprises they had for us.

Of course, we were always caught. I've learned a lot since I was a girl, though, so no point getting stressed about that. Especially after working with Cynthia. She's one clever spell caster.

As much as I'd love to continue reliving these memories, I force them away. This is no time for nostalgia. Clear and peaceful. Nothing but the task at hand.

I gather my magic and oh so slowly, it winds from my hand toward the spot underneath the table where the legs meet. A tiny, tucked away corner. As it reaches the spot, I think of Zade, of the sound of his voice. The warm, comforting sound of a friend. The harsh temper of a protective big brother. The ache of him telling me his fears.

All of it comes out, tinting the clear spell with yellows, reds, and blues. Thankfully, they're faint colors. Once I set the spell to remain off until his voice activates, the colors will disappear until then.

Once everything is securely in place, I release the spell. Its colors die off, hopefully ready to activate when needed. That's should do—

"What are you doing under there?" An all too familiar voice booms, making me jerk upright and hit my head on the underside of the table.

"Ow." Pain throbs through my forehead.

"Oh, it's you," Jack says.

With each word, my head pounds more. Not only do I wish he'd never entered the room and almost caught me doing something that would get me, at best, killed, but now I wish he'd just go away so the stabbing sensation wouldn't be as bad.

"Yes, it's me," I say as I scoot out from under the table. "At least, what's left of me after you startled me into smacking my forehead. What made you think it'd be a good idea to scare me while I'm trying to get the cleaning done?"

"You're cleaning?" One of his eyebrows raises like he doesn't believe me. Given the nature of what I was doing, I can't blame him. I do anyway. Brute.

"Yes, I'm cleaning. Don't you know there's a council meeting tomorrow?"

"Everyone is aware."

"Well then, why were you yelling at me while I was trying to clean?"

"Because climbing under the table isn't necessary to clean well. Is this some strange ritual that takes place in Envadi culture?"

Strange Envadi ritual indeed. He probably hates warm milk, too. "Don't you ever clean the floors under there? And the…" I struggle to think of a legitimate reason why I'd be down here on the floor. "…chairs? Look at the seats and legs of these things. There's an alarming amount of grime."

His eyes narrow. Definitely not buying my story. But my spell isn't active yet and won't be until Zade's voice sets it off, so barring that, it's not like he can find anything wrong.

To prove my story, I lean back down and rub my cloth from cleaning the windows down the legs of the closest chair. It actually is kind of gross this close up. Not awful, but like no one's really thought of this task before. Still, as I move to the next leg, it feels rather inane, but I don't stop. The carving parts where there's more of a crevice in the chair have the most amount of dust, which takes the most work to clean out. I push harder at slipping my rag into each one like these chairs really need to be shiny for tomorrow. The whole time I'm focusing in on him while he looks at the chair, trying to gauge his reaction. Wondering if he believes my story.

It doesn't take long to forget about him as I come to a crevice that's particularity deep. When I finally get it clean, I realize I forgot to keep track of him and glance up. He rolls his eyes.

There. He's bought my story, even if it meant making a fool of myself; it's nothing new where he's concerned. Without another word, he strides from the room. I won't miss him when it comes time to leave and find a place I can help more. Too bad it's not today. Even more unfortunate now, I have to scrub all these chairs. All fifteen of them. That's a lot of chair legs. What a foolish way to spend my afternoon. Tomorrow had better be worth it.

I'm just finishing the first chair when Jack comes striding back in the room. What trouble is he going to cause now? Except he doesn't say a word, or even look at me. He sits on the floor next to me, pulls out a cloth, and starts wiping down the chair.

Is this guy for real? Does he want to help get these clean or is this a way of keeping an eye on me? It has to be the latter. There's no other reason someone like him could possibly have for doing otherwise.

I move on to the next chair on the other side, working on cleaning out each crack. It's mind- numbing work that leaves room for thought, but instead my mind clears, making way for just the movement to lull me in a sort of peace I haven't felt for a long while.

Time quickly passes as we work, and we continue to move away from each other until we're half way through and we start moving toward one another. By the time I get to the last chair, my arms ache. While I'm working on the front legs, Jack takes the back until we're both through.

I drag myself to a standing position and stretch my arms far above my head and then behind my back. It feels good to move about after being cramped on the floor so long. And it would have been longer if it wasn't for Jack. Grudgingly I say, "Thank you—"

"Don't bother," he interrupts. "If I hadn't helped, you would have still been here when the warlocks arrived to secure it for the meeting, which would cause problems and delays."

Meaning, I cause problems and delays, but it answers why he helped. At least he doesn't suspect me of something.

"And if they find anything," he eyes the table where I left the spell, "you can be assured they will know who did it."

Or not. "I'm sure they'll do an excellent job."

He glares me down as if that will somehow make me stop talking. "You need to lower your face to me."

These warlocks really have no clue how to treat a female. I laugh even though I feel more like slapping him. "Why would I do such a thing?"

"Because you are a woman."

"I most definitely am." I make certain to look him right in the eyes, letting all the fierceness boiling within me shine through them. "And you sir, are a man with very poor manners."

I turn away, but before I'm able to escape past him entirely, he has the gall to say, "We run a better house than this. You will follow Chardonian rules while you're here. Learn them and don't dawdle again. If you're faced with a task that time-consuming, request help."

It wouldn't have been any time at all if he hadn't interrupted. "Whatever. I'm just doing my job."

I brush past him, my arm tingling as it grazes his. Chardonian warlocks! Really, what gives them any idea they can treat people like this? I dealt with it when I was here before, but most of the time, it was secondhand stories from the girls. Rarely was I in a place where it happened directly to me.

Despite his warning to me, it doesn't make me want to change my own behavior. It only makes me want to work harder at changing his.

CHAPTER 11

"I hope you two ladies don't mind, but Daniel wanted to spend the evening with me," Annabelle says.

I halt my forward movement into her room and instead take a step back. "We can visit some other night, then."

"Don't leave on my account," Councilman Daniel says. "Please stay a while. I wouldn't mind getting to know you both better. Annabelle has only good things to say of each of you."

Another excuse is about to spill from my mouth so we don't intrude on their time together when Tawny says, "If you insist, I suppose we will have to. I must admit, I've been curious to learn more about you as well, since Annabelle speaks of you so often and highly, Councilman."

Often? We've only been here four days. But there's no getting out of it now. I take a chair across from the Councilman and his wife. Tawny pours tea for them, asking the Councilman how he would like his but adjusting Annabelle's without question. She then pours a cup of warm milk for us and sits beside me.

"Tawny talks with me often," Annabelle says. "But what about you, Waverly? How are you adjusting to life here?"

I take a sip and try not to scrunch my nose. It tastes burned but is lukewarm. I'll have to see if I can spend some time in the kitchens if I remain here and teach them the proper way to prepare a cup of milk. Whatever this stuff is, it's not at all soothing.

"It's like coming home for me. A different house than I was in before, but still home."

"You don't find our ways backwards, then?" the Councilman asks.

Time to tread carefully. He may be on our side, but he's still on the council. "They are definitely different than where I'm from. I find many of your people endearing and some others who..." I'd like to punch in the nose. "...aren't as much."

He laughs. "A good political answer. Don't worry, I don't like a lot of the people here either, but it's home for us too. We're doing what we can to help with that. When we can get around the Grand Chancellor, that is."

I don't think any of us realized just how good of allies Annabelle and Daniel are. We should have. I'm excited just thinking of adding their help. "How has that been going for you?"

"Lately, people have been more open to speaking with me about changing things. It's been wonderful to see. Unfortunately, the Grand Chancellor knows it and continues clamping down on as many laws as he can."

"Isn't there more you can do?" Tawny asks. I'm sure this is harder for her to hear than it is to me. I'm used to this, as much as I don't want to be. She's used to how Envado rules.

"I wish there was, but I'm just a voice in a large crowd. One the Grand Chancellor doesn't have to listen to."

"You do a good job, my dear," Annabelle says.

He takes a hold of her hand as he continues. "It wasn't always this way, you know. There was a time when the council was actually a council that worked together with the Grand Chancellor. Too many years with too many men grabbing for as much power as they can, has left the position of Grand Chancellor with too much weight."

"Do you think anything can be done about it?" I ask. Because there has to be. If not, all of this will be for not.

"As things are, I don't know. The Grand Chancellor keeps making things stricter and stricter. At this rate, the entire country will be on lock down unless you're Chancellor Ryan or Councilman Stephen."

"What? I though Chancellor Ryan was kicked off the council after the tournament when he forced Nathaniel to take the magic from those women. And Stephen hasn't been on since Serena's ball when he tried to have Zade murdered."

"I'm afraid the Grand Chancellor has reinstated them both."

"But he got rid of Chancellor Ryan because of the effect he was going to have on relationships with other countries. Doesn't he care about that still?"

Daniel sighs. "Apparently, not any longer."

"How are we going to hold any leverage against him if he doesn't care what other countries think?" Tawny says.

"We'll just have to keep trying different things," he replies.

Annabelle yawns. "Excuse me. I'm not used to staying up to this hour."

"It's getting late," I say with a yawn of my own.

"I'm afraid time got away from us," Annabelle says as we all stand. "Thank you for joining us this evening, Waverly."

"I was happy to. It was great getting to know you both better. I really appreciate your candidness."

"Anytime," Daniel says.

As I pull the door shut behind me, I catch a last glimpse of Annabelle and Daniel, still sitting side by side holding hands, but now gazing at each other, perfectly content just to be in one another's presence. If only we could get this country to be so content with everyone else in it. There has to be a way to rid the country of the Grand Chancellor's poison.

CHAPTER 12

The council meeting should have started by now. I pace the short length of my room, wishing there was more space to really stretch my legs. What if they somehow figured out how to catch my spell before it activated? They are council members after all. They're supposed to be some of the best warlocks in Chardonia, even if the Grand Chancellors, throughout the ages, have taken away their power. Though I'm not sure if the "best" means the ones with the most power or the ones with the most influence. Either way, it's daunting to think about.

What's more, it's not just the councilmen I need to worry about. There's Chancellor Ryan and Zade who are a bigger threat. Zade would be even more livid than Chancellor Ryan at my scheme. Though Chancellor Ryan would probably torture or kill me, while Zade would just yell. Brothers.

And then there's the Grand Chancellor. He's not a warlock I want discovering I'm trying to spy on him. What if he decides to make me his next sacrifice?

I shake my head. Stupid, useless thoughts. I'm not a tarnished, the council won't sacrifice me. Of course, that doesn't mean they won't find some other form of punishment. Or that they won't tarnish me and then sacrifice me. It won't matter. I'm still an Envadi while I'm in their lands; that much has been made very clear.

Gah. All this time in Chardonia is wearing on me. Making me worry over things I shouldn't. Next thing I know, I'll be lowering my head to Jack.

My pacing grows more frantic. I need more useful thoughts. Something that isn't driven by fear. What is useful to think about? The spell hasn't been activated, so it's like it's not even there. And how could they discover it if it's not working? Would they even know it's from me? Or would they think it's from Councilman Daniel? Maybe he's getting in trouble for it right now. I can't bring that on him. Not before, but especially not after, chatting with him last night. He and his wife are much too good to deserve something like that to befall them.

I direct my pacing toward the door to break the rule of going out there to see what's happened when my fingers finally tingle. The spell is working. They didn't find it after all.

I sag with relief onto the chair. Unless of course they found the spell and purposefully made Zade activate it to try and discover who cast it. I sit ramrod straight.

No sense waiting to see if they come after me. I cast the second half of the spell that allows me to hear what's being said by thinking of the first half of the spell and Zade's voice. Zade must have spoken already because my finger is now tingling. I hold my colored finger up to my ear.

"...has been brought to my attention." The Grand Chancellor is speaking, I think. "More Envadi have entered our country. Without clearance."

Though this discussion does sound like it's my fault, at least it's not related to the spell.

"This is a serious problem, indeed," someone replies but I don't know who. Not having sight is more frustrating than I suspected.

"Indeed." The Grand Chancellor again. "Not only have they

entered, but they have received aid from at least two members of this council."

Zade and Councilman Daniel! Oh lands, what have I done? They're the ones who helped Tawny and I. Now they're going to get in trouble because of my insistence on coming back here, even when Zade said it was unsafe. I just never thought he meant unsafe for them.

"New measures have to be taken. I will no longer try to appease the community as a whole, or other countries. It's time to do what's best for Chardonia no matter the consequences that befall because of it." The Grand Chancellor makes it sound as if he's a martyr in all this. Jerk. "Hence forth, the following will apply, and I will not hear anyone utter a word until it's settled."

I begin pacing again, all the while holding my spelled finger up to my ear. My gut churns.

"First, no woman shall be allowed the status of a warlock, no matter what. No law shall impede this one. Nothing shall allow them this status unfitting of simple property."

My heart clenches as someone tries to speak, but I can't make out the muffled words.

"Silence!" The Grand Chancellor's yell is so firm, it makes my ear ache. "There is not room for arguments, Chancellor, as I previously stated. Furthermore, your arguments will be moot shortly."

That does not sound good. Not at all. A chill runs through me as I grab my pack, throwing things into it the best I can with one hand while he continues.

"In accordance with this first rule, no woman will be allowed to practice magic. Ever. Anyone caught aiding them with this in *any* way will immediately be put to death. There will be no more erasing memories spell. Punishment shall be swift, harsh, and unfailingly public."

My stomach churns as I grab a pack for Tawny as well. Whatever happens, whether or not they catch my spell, we need to leave. We pushed the Grand Chancellor too far to not have further repercussions, and he knows we're here. All the work we've done working with the people, will it be enough to counter this new law or will it scare those already frightened souls? What will happen to everyone who supports us now? Who was thinking of supporting us?

"Not only that, but because of the nature of these crimes taking place and the unprecedented amount of trouble and change happening recently, all Council members will be held to these laws as well. Any of you who break them in the future will suffer the same punishment."

I fall into a chair, packs tumbling to the ground. A stunned sort of stupor comes over me.

There's a murmur from several warlocks, but I can't tell what they're saying, if it's good or bad. How much worse could it possibly get? How will Zade survive this change? The Grand Chancellor doesn't say a word against the murmurs, just continues on with his mad plan.

"From this moment, the council is banned. Chancellor Ryan will remain along with the new Chancellor Stephen."

Curse those scum.

"Those of you who have served me faithfully will, of course, be rewarded and will be given positions elsewhere as new laws go into effect. We will need your skills and loyalty to help with any... disturbances resulting from the changes so things can settle as soon as possible. Furthermore, anyone on this council who has broken these new laws at any previous moment will be arrested, imprisoned, and tortured until the next tournament when they will be put to death in front of not just our own citizens, but those of other countries."

Zade! I jump up, knocking my chair to the floor.

There are several loud crashes followed by the Grand Chancellor, his voice almost gleeful. "Ah-ah Envadi. You've been so kind as to try and free our women, it's only fair you let us now show you our hospitality." There's another loud crash. "You too, Daniel. We can't be soft on our own countryman, now can we?"

Icy torrents blare through me. Zade's already captured. Daniel's already captured. What do I do? Nothing prepared me for this. No amount of preparing to get caught working a spell, nothing. I flex my hand, dashing for the door.

My efforts will not be in vain. I can't save Zade and Daniel on my own, but there may be a chance to save others. And come back for them once I have a specific plan.

CHAPTER 13

I sprint from my room, thinking about Serena. She has to be told immediately. Please don't let the Grand Chancellor be prepared to take her out before I have time to warn her. They have to have enough time. Her guards had better be there and remember what to do in a time such as this. I draft the message and spell it to go to her house as quickly as I can while on the run. It darts down the hall and out of sight. I plead silently with it that it doesn't get interrupted. It's more imperative now than ever before.

It's hard not knowing for sure what the Grand Chancellor would do. Would he count on being able to stop Zade from spreading the word? Or would he be more prepared than that?

My legs ache as I burst up the stairs. Stupid time to have them so sore from yesterday, being curled up cleaning. If it saves Annabelle and Tawny, though, it will be worth even more pain than this burn. Just beyond horrid. If only I can get to them in time.

Is there going to be an "in time?" Or would the Grand Chancellor already have had plans in place to take her out from the change he just made? The thought urges me on faster, but as quietly as I can go.

I slow as I come to the last hall. I peek around the corner and dart back. There are two warlocks standing outside Annabelle's room.

Double foiled.

Can I take these two down myself? And what if there are more inside? They could hear if I'm not careful. It's what I get for spending too much time spelling my nails. Do I try it or not? Maybe it's too late. If I get captured with them, who will know to bring help? There's nothing I can do for them now. Not without endangering myself. I take a step toward the stairs, but immediately pull back and blast a sleep spell, channeling all of my energy and focusing on it just the way Cynthia would.

They fall to the ground, out cold. Today is not the day to be a wuss. At least, so far. There could be more problems along the way. Besides, I can't bring help. I am the help.

I tiptoe down the hall as quickly as I can. The guards are perfectly still on the ground other than their breathing. Good. I'm not Cynthia though, so who knows how long they'll be out.

It's time to face whatever's in there. After several deep breaths, I open the door and stride in, closing it behind me like I'm supposed to be there. Not that guards would believe a woman was sent to do anything important, but if I at least pretend, maybe I could be another prisoner?

As I take in the room, there's good news and bad. No guard inside. Unfortunately, Jack is. He's sitting next to Annabelle and Tawny as they all hold teacups, giving me a funny look.

Is he there for the Grand Chancellor, or does he have some other purpose? There's no time to find out. I raise my hands toward him.

"Waverly!" Annabelle shouts. "What are you doing?"

Too late. Jack is on his guard now, his tea splashed all over the floor. His hands are up, ready to cast a spell against me.

"Annabelle," I say, trying to keep my voice calm. "We need to go. Now."

"What is going on here?" she asks. "Both of you stop threatening the other this instant."

I don't take my eyes from Jack, and there's not time to answer Annabelle. "Are you here because of the Grand Chancellor?"

"What are you going on about?" The confusion on his face looks real, but he could be a very good actor.

"The Grand Chancellor?" Annabelle asks.

"We don't have time for this," I say. "Zade and Daniel have been arrested and sentenced to death. The council has been disbanded. There were guards outside your door, and I don't know how long we have until more come."

"Jack, check the hall." Annabelle's command surprises me.

I keep my hands raised at him as he moves toward me, but let him pass, taking the opportunity to get closer to Annabelle and Tawny, who is remaining sensibly quiet. Though insensibly hasn't tried to help me threaten Jack yet.

Jack turns his back to me, and I *almost* hex him, but Annabelle knocks my hands to the side. I glare at her. "I'm trying to keep you safe."

"So is he."

"Two, of them," Jack says. "I gave them an extra sleep spell, but there's no telling how long it will last."

Annabelle moves without hesitation, but instead of toward the hall like I expect, to a wardrobe.

"We don't have time to grab anything." Even the bags I so carefully packed for Tawny and me are still on the floor of our room. Drat my not grabbing them.

She pulls open the wardrobe and slips the back panel off to reveal a hidden path. "There's already some packs ready."

They already have a plan in place for something such as this? I should have known. "What about him?" I motion to Jack.

"I'm coming with you."

"I think not."

"He's coming," Annabelle says. "Don't you dare hex him."

Why is this woman so attached to him? He's rude. "He'll turn us in."

There's a shuffling out in the hall. Not close, but not far enough away either.

"There's no time to argue. Everyone get in, and I'll close it behind us." Annabelle scampers inside, waiting just inside the passage.

She can't really be letting him come with us.

Jack closes the door to her room and stacks some chairs against it while Tawny darts into the passage to where I can no longer see her. He moves toward the passage as well, and I let him. I guess Jack is coming with us. Doesn't mean I'm not ready to drop him a hex at a moment's notice, though.

I hurry in after them, and Annabelle puts the panel back on the wardrobe.

"Do you want any sort of spell on it?" I ask.

"No. It would probably just draw their attention here more."

True. She's clearly thought about this escape a lot more than I have.

We hurry down the tunnel, attempting to keep our steps quiet, which isn't an easy feat at such a rapid pace in the dark on a rock path.

There's a muffled bang behind us, followed by several more. They must be breaking into Annabelle's room. My heart clenches. Now's not the time for losing it. I have to keep them safe. I have to. We can't go to all this trouble only to be caught.

It's hard to focus on my steps, to think of where we're going, when at any moment they could discover the secret passage. The noise behind us, while still muffled, grows louder. We move faster, using the noise to cover our own. My nerves feel as if they're trying to jump out of me.

We come to a set of stairs that Annabelle warns us of. It's hard to use them in the dark, but once we've gone down a ways, Annabelle stops and lights a torch. The tunnel is made of dirt, stone steps beneath our feet and wooden beams above our heads. We continue to wind our way down them, the noise fading with every step. I want to think we're out of danger, that we've made it, but we're still in the same house as them. There's far to go.

A few tunnels branch off the main corridor, but Annabelle continues down the main path, twisting, turning, and descending. Soon the walls have roots growing out of them. It grows cool, the crisp air a welcome contrast to my hot skin.

Annabelle looks back every so often to make certain we're all still following, but otherwise, we press on through what must be an underground passage. The fact that there's been passages off of the main tunnel makes me more confident we won't be found. That we might just make it.

The passage comes to a room with several packs in it, blankets, and a ladder leading up.

"Everyone grab a pack. We should be hidden by the forest out here, but we will check to make certain it's clear before coming out."

"I'll peek," I volunteer.

"Let me," Jack says, but I'm already climbing the ladder.

I'm sure he would, and then declare our presence to the enemy if the opportunity presents itself. He's a Chardonian warlock. What else would he possibly want to do? So while staying quiet and careful, I hurry to open the door on the roof. I crack it open, just a pinch. There's nothing in sight but trees and a squirrel.

"I think we're clear. Let me check for certain. If I don't return within ten minutes, stay here and be prepared for anything."

With the borrowed pack on my back, I check one final time before escaping out into the world. I glance around at the cleverly hidden trap door and make note of what it looks like so I can find it again.

I creep as quietly as I can. Mom and Dad didn't teach us stealth for nothing. The immediate area is clear of anyone except me, but I don't trust it. There's nothing but trees in sight. We must be in the forest near the house, though it isn't in sight.

The woods are so quiet. I slink around it. Maybe none of the warlocks from the house suspect us to be out here yet. And they wouldn't realize we'd make a break for it, so they didn't set up guards outside the perimeter. Or if they did, they'd still be looking for us at the house.

I suppose it's possible, but it doesn't fit with what I know of the Grand Chancellor. Especially with such changes like those he just made. And with Zad— I can't allow my thoughts any further down that path. Now is not the time to lose it.

I'm just about to return to the others when a flash of bright green catches my eye. I dart behind the nearest tree, wait a moment, then peek around it. A warlock all right. A guard from the way he's scanning the scene. Yet clearly not doing a good enough job since he hasn't noticed me yet. Over-confidence in others is a blessing in times like these.

I follow him silently for several minutes. He tracks first north then south, passing by the original spot I saw him. When he heads back, I figure this must be the area he's in charge of and since I haven't seen anyone else, silencing him would be best.

Instinct says to spell him, only with my skill level, I can't guarantee it will work for long. Best knock him out the old fashioned way, I guess.

After finding the biggest rock I can, I hide behind a tree and wait for him to go past. Only he doesn't move past. Where is he? There's a crunch of leaves. Here he comes. I grip the rock tight in my hand and whirl around the tree, arm raised high. I bring the rock down only to realize there is no guard, only Jack.

Oh well. I continue to bring my arm down anyway.

He sidesteps, grabs my arm, and shoves it toward the ground, making me drop the rock. "You took too long getting back. I already took out the guard."

I huff at him. Almost had the guard and him taken care of. Annabelle better know what she's doing trusting him. Though I hate to do so, Mother did instill manners in me. I let out a gruff, "Thank you."

I twirl away from him and hurry back to Annabelle and Tawny. My breathing is uneven as I return to the hidden spot. I lift the hatch. They're patiently waiting in the hidden room. "It's safe now. Are they going to be able to track you through any of the things you left behind?"

Jack and Tawny should know what I'm talking about, but I expect to need to explain it to Annabelle, but she says, "Daniel spelled all of my things long ago not to be attached to me. They won't be able to spell any of my items to find us."

"He's not at all like other Chardonian warlocks."

"No, he isn't. One of the biggest reasons he worked so hard to get on the council and to gain supporters was to fight against the Grand Chancellor." Her voice cracks. "And now it's the reason he's gained a death sentence."

Tawny and I both give her a quick hug. It's all there's time for. It sounds like Daniel prepared for something like this to happen, but not being separated from the wife he so clearly cherishes.

"I forgot our packs, Tawny."

"All my important things were back home."

"And I have nothing of importance, so my things won't be a problem," Jack adds.

If I wasn't so worried about him turning on us, I'd feel sad for him. Everyone should have at least one thing of importance. And why wouldn't a Chardonian warlock have something like that?

"I'm like Tawny and left my important things back in Envado," I say. "Thank you for having these packs ready for us, Annabelle. They'll be vital. Let's go."

We're walking for maybe five minutes when I hear a noise. I stop and put my hand up in the air. The others go instantly silent. There's a crunch close by to the right. That had better be some sort of animal. Another crunch follows and another, sounding all too much like the footsteps of a person. Drat.

I glance toward where the sound is coming from. There's a flash of black. A law officer. Just what we don't need. With a little luck, he'll walk right by us without noticing our presence. I hold my breath as he continues by. And he keeps going. We've made it.

Suddenly, the man looks back, staring straight into my eyes. I don't think, just react, slamming a punching spell into him, the bright black and green smashing into him twice more. He falls back.

"Run."

The others take off after me, Jack bringing up the rear. There's no time to think whether or not this is going to work against us. There's more crashing through the brush coming our way. The disturbance must have attracted more attention.

A burgundy spell comes flying at us. Before I can react, Jack stops it with a canary yellow spell of his own. The spells clash in a burst of color while we put on more speed to get away from them. I'm not sure if Annabelle can keep up with us, but she surprises me by running faster than me, pulling to the front of the group.

"Is there any way to tell if there's someone ahead of us?" she calls out.

"Yes." I send a spell out, a soft yellow, searching for any hints of the heat of people ahead of us. Nothing. "I think the way is clear. Keep going."

We run, my legs burning with the effort. Four more spells zip at us from behind, but each one is fainter than the last. We're going to make it.

Out of nowhere, a midnight-blue spell crashes into me, knocking me to the ground and sending chills through me. Tawny stands over me like an avenging warrior, a purple spell streaked with pink screaming from her.

There's a cry followed by silences.

Annabelle checks me over for injuries. I tell her I'm fine, and she helps me stand.

"There's no time to linger," Jack says.

Even though he's right, I glare at him. We hurry to get moving again, running for a good half-an-hour before Annabelle declares she can't keep going any longer. We slow to a walk but keep moving.

Lost them. Possibly. Hopefully. I motion for everyone to keep quiet as we continue. Our trail is all too easy to follow with a tracking spell, despite everyone stepping cautiously. Even a simple warlock could cast a spell to find the trail of footprints we're leaving.

I try to cast a spell to hide our path. The tan light covers some of our footprints, but not all the way. I've never had a talent for it like Chadwick does. His hiding spells are like works of art, mine a clumsy smudge of mess. This isn't the best way for me to help. It isn't even really helping.

What am I going to do with Annabelle and the others? How am I to keep them all safe? Not only am I struggling to hide our tracks, there's nowhere to take them that is safe except Envado. I suppose I could try and take them there and return, but I doubt they'll be happy about leaving instead of fighting. Especially since I told them all that Zade and Daniel were captured. Jack should be the only one who won't care about their release. Well, maybe Councilman Daniel's since he is keeping him out of debt.

But will Zade and Daniel still be themselves after all that time? What exactly did the Grand Chancellor mean when he said...this isn't something I want to think on. I can't think on it. Not now.

Jack huffs, pulling me from my morbid thoughts.

"What?" I whisper yell at him.

"Your spell casting skills are dismal."

Only because it's not a pampering spell. "Like you could do any better."

The corners of his mouth tighten. He casts the spell, the

muddy light wiping away all of evidence of us being there, fixing broken branches, filling in dirt, and fluffing the bits of vegetation.

He glares me down.

"It's a good spell," I admit.

He cocks an eyebrow at me, and suddenly, I'm aware of how golden his eyes are. It's a nice distraction from all the stress, but not at all helpful. I've got to figure out what our next step is.

I hurry on, letting him take care of our tracks while I try to focus on where to go and forget those piercing eyes. I've got to get a note to Cynthia. She's not as urgent as Serena, but she still needs to know as soon as possible. I wish there was a way to know how Serena is doing, but all I can do is hope she's safe. If I try to find out, I could give her location away or distract her when she needs to focus.

But Cynthia, that I can take care of now. I zap a spell note that's mostly clear with bits of yellow scattered through it. Thinking of the hideout she should be at now, I push it her way. I hope she knows what to do. Me, I haven't a clue. But there is a safe house not far from here by some of my fellow Envadi's Sanos, the group that's been helping Chardonians.

"What did you do?" Jack's voices snaps at me like a spell gone wrong.

"What are you so upset about?"

"What spell did you just cast? Are you trying to bring those warlocks down on us? Anyone looking this way could have seen it. You are trying to get us killed."

"Course I'm not, you brute. I'm trying to save more lives than just yours."

His face changes at my words. Softens just the tiniest fraction. Maybe, just maybe, I've found a weakness. But probably not.

"You might want to warn those you need to as well," I say.

The defensive look is immediately back. "And get us killed in the process? I don't think so. Besides, the only person I know doesn't need to be warned about anything. And you shouldn't send any more spells either."

I scoff and want to throw a good retort, except he's right. I was going to warn Katherine so she would know and tell other tarnished what's taking place, but she's not in immediate danger. At least so much so that it's worth risking the lives of those I'm with. Once we're sure that we're not being watched, I can send them out. I have to put the lives of those I'm with first. Even if it feels totally wrong not to warn the whole of Chardonia and Envado.

To tell Mom and Dad what's happened.

My throat chokes up. Time to get back to the spell I sent out. I mumble, "It was only one spell and barely visible at that."

He seems to think I'm not going to cast anymore because he doesn't say another word. For now. We follow Annabelle until we reach a tree with three trunks.

"This is where Daniel told me to go if there was ever a problem and he wasn't here to help."

The area is a bit of a nook. There's a giant rock and some thick trees helping to hide us from prying eyes, but we're too close to the patrol group for me to feel any comfort. We're not safe here at all.

"Was there some place you were to go after this?" Jack asks. Surprisingly, he must be thinking along the same lines.

"Nowhere. He said he would come and get me."

"So we wait?" Tawny asks.

Jack looks at me, and I know we're thinking the same thing, though why he's suddenly sharing the moment with me, I don't know. It's too much like an Envadi male thing and not at all like a Chardonian. I adjust my pack, wondering if I should bring up the fact that he's not going to be coming for her, even though she should know it.

"I think that…" The words choke my throat closed. It's not just Daniel that isn't coming for her.

"I know." Annabelle is looking back toward her home, though it's been a long time since we were able to see it.

I force the words past the emotion clogging my throat. "We need to keep moving."

"Where to?" Tawny asks, like I'm supposed to know everything about Chardonia after being here just over a year.

"There's a place we can go and be sort of safe. Other Chardonian's may be there to help or we should be able to contact them, but it's a few days' journey from here on foot." That is, if we continue to make it without being caught.

Jack shakes his head like I'm useless at this, which I am, but still. "Follow me."

"I don't think so," I reply.

Annabelle finally turns her gaze away from the direction of her house and onto me, giving me a strange look. "He knows his way around this area very well. He's explored it since he came to work for us several years ago. It would be wise to follow him."

I grit my teeth and keep my eyes focused on the group though the ground seems much more appealing at the moment. It is strange to think about Jack coming to work when he was so young. He's probably only a year older than me. "Well then, Jack, lead the way. The place I need to take us is north of here. Do you have somewhere in mind that way?"

"Just try to keep up."

Like he can't even give a real response. Why bother when we're just women? If he starts taking us farther away, I swear I'm putting this thing to a stop and making my own way with Tawny and Annabelle, dragging them along whether they'd like to or not. I pull my magic from my core, out to the tips of my fingers, ready to zap him with whatever I need to should he turn on us.

CHAPTER 14

T he whole process is much smoother than I expect. Even if
he is a Chardonian warlock, Jack doesn't seem intent on
turning us in to the Grand Chancellor. For now. The whole way
he's been quiet and watchful, even helping Annabelle and Tawny
over fallen trees when they needed a hand. Fine, he probably
would have helped me too, but I'm too busy keeping an eye on
him to let him get so close to me.

Still, he's done a much better job at not just leading but is nicer
than I expected. Who knows what the world is coming to? We
continue our walk until suddenly Jack freezes and motions for us
to stay back.

"What is it?" I whisper. But then he doesn't have to reply
because I see it. A brown, baby bear cub, not four feet from where
we're standing. What's she doing out all on her own?

"Back up quietly," Jack says.

We begin to do so, taking steps slowly and carefully. Still, I
can't take my eyes off the baby bear. There's a growl from the
woods, close. Now we're in for it.

"Keep going," he insists when I stop.

As much as I don't want to meet momma bear, I don't know if running from her is the best option either.

Jack presses his back into me, pushing me toward the other. I want to swat him to make him stop, but momma bear appears, snarling directly at us.

Panic strikes me, but there is no time to let it. I have to think and act fast. The bear comes running for us. Make that thinking faster.

Just before she gets to us, I manage a spell that creates a wall between us and her. She slams against it, growling.

"Hurry," I demand. "I don't know how long I can hold this up."

We run. The bear is livid, smashing against the spelled wall. What's worse than just the bear is all the noise she's making. It could easily give away our position to the warlocks chasing us. My hope is that they can't hear her, and if they can that they don't want to investigate why an animal is so upset.

The bear crashes through my spell. "She's coming!"

"Keep going," Jack yells. "I'll hold her off."

Like I'm going to let him protect us all. What if he fails? Maybe I should let him fail and then help, but I just can't bring myself to do it. I turn and stop with him.

"Go!" he yells.

Ignoring him, I cast a spell that's all light hovering around Jack and I, making us look bigger with bright yellow and orange lights. Jack adds to my idea casting a green-lighted spell to my own.

The bear slows.

"That's right you bear," I yell. "Get away from us. Go back to your baby. Shoo now. Go on, shoo!"

"Don't look her in the eye," he hollers over my shouts.

I immediately drop my gaze while keeping up my hollering and spell. She saunters forward still, but I don't move. I stand my ground, hollering gibberish. Beside me, Jack is speaking to the bear in a calm tone. At least I'm not the only one crazy enough to speak to the bear.

Finally, the bear moves slower and slower until she turns around and heads back toward her cub. I immediately stop shouting. What have I done? I hope I haven't called the warlocks to us with all my noise, but it seems effective. The bear is no longer in sight. I drop my spell, but I don't drop my gaze from where the bear left.

"Let's go," Jack says, heading directly left of where the bear went. "Waverly, take the rear. We've got to move fast to not only get away from the bear, but away from here in case the law officers heard."

I want to fight him, but I don't dare. Not with what just happened. Someone needs to protect Annabelle and Tawny's backs. I just wish there was someone to protect mine.

"I hope I never see another bear again," Annabelle says.

"I'll second that," I reply.

We continue hurrying through the area like the bear is chasing us. I don't think we want to take any chances. We walk several more hours until Jack stops leading us and is lazily wandering into a clearing that has nothing in it and is surrounded by trees and bushes coming over a mountain. It seems he is ignoring us and has all the time in the world to lollygag.

"Is it time for a break?" Or have you just gone mad?

Though his body language ignores me, he says, "Just making sure we weren't being followed, at least not by someone close by."

Oh, he's good. "Which means you don't trust your own spell to keep our tracks hidden."

"Which means I'm cautious because I don't want to lead them to a safe hiding spot."

Fine. But just because he's being smart for the moment, doesn't mean I have to trust him. Tawny and Annabelle have no problem as they talk quietly to each other. I'm sure I could join them, but I'm just so used to keeping an eye on Chardonian warlocks, I can't bring myself to chat.

Finally, he moves to a group of vines off to one side of the clearing. It was hard for me to pick them out with so much other foliage about. Underneath is a dark, narrow opening.

"Are there any critters living in it?" I ask.

"Why don't you go see? If there are any, I'm certain you can scare them away for us."

I raise my head and, without giving him a second glance, I stride into the cave. So what if there's a mama bear protecting her cubs? I can take it, though once I'm in, I release some of my magic in a burst to light the way. After moving through a narrow tunnel, a wide cavern opens up. Relief floods through me that there's no mama bear, or any other animal in sight.

I make sure to scout the entire area. It's not big, but big enough to suit our needs. Once I'm certain there's nothing here but dirt and rocks, I lower my hand.

"Did the critters frighten you?" Jack says as he enters the cave.

"Only as much as you do."

"How did you find this?" Tawny asks him.

He shrugs. "Like Annabelle said, I've explored around here often."

Once everyone is in and the vines are back in place from the outside, I collapse to the floor, using my pack as a pillow. "That was exhausting."

"If we weren't running for our lives, it would have been a good vigorous walk," Jack says.

I glare at him. But the running for our lives reminds me of why we're here, and now that I'm not distracted by keeping track of our surroundings, it's impossible not to think on Zade.

Where is he? Is he in a lot of pain? Are they torturing him?

I squeeze my eyes shut tight, trying to keep composure. What is Serena going to do when she finds out how serious things are for Zade? I told her to run, told her to get out of there as fast as she could and that Zade was in trouble. But I didn't say how bad things really are for him. I don't even want to think how bad they are. What the Grand Chancellor could do.

Across from me, Annabelle is silent, her eyes closed, but I doubt she's sleeping. At least I didn't tell her everything, and that she doesn't know how serious it actually is. Torture. That's what the Grand Chancellor said.

How am I possibly going to save my brother from torture?

CHAPTER 15

I don't know when I fall asleep, but it's followed by much fitfulness. At least I manage to get some sleep in. By the heavy bags under Annabelle's eyes, it appears she had a lot more problems than I did.

"Can we make it to your safe house today?" Jack asks, handing me some dried meat.

The action startles me until I see Tawny pull out more and hand it to him and then hand some to Annabelle. "I'm not sure exactly where we are," I admit.

He casts a spell in front of us that looks like a map, only made out of colored lights instead of paper. It's a spell I've seen from far away before but never up close. It has detail and talent.

"Councilman Daniel's house is here. We traveled this path yesterday." His finger traces a line on the glowing map.

It's easy to tell where the safe house should be, but I don't want to trust him with its location. The thing is, he did bring us here, and his spell to hide our tracks seems to have worked since no one has found us yet. Plus, he didn't turn us over to the guards when he had the chance.

Besides, as much as I don't think I want to think of the possibility, something could happen to me. Zade's loss has taught me that much. I have to trust him.

"We should be able to make it to there even if we don't run into any trouble along the way." I hesitate only another second before pointing to the spot on his spell where the closest safe house is. I can only hope it's still safe after everything that's happened.

"I'm certain we can make it." The soft but serious tone of his voice makes me feel like I was right to trust him. I only hope he doesn't betray that trust.

"How soon can everyone be ready to go?"

Annabelle jumps to her feet. "As soon as needed."

The ache in her gaze makes my own heart wrench to the ground. As soon as they're safe, I'll do what I can to help Zade and Daniel.

Tawny is still eating but bounces to her feet as well, dried meat in hand. "Let's go."

I nod to Jack who leads us out of the cave and then arranges the vines and grounds carefully after we're all back in the clearing.

He moves next to me but seems to have trouble saying anything.

After several moments of silence, I say, "Is there something you needed?"

His jaw tenses and relaxes several times. "Would you like to lead us today?"

He's offering? And not just offering, but offering without any sort of cajoling? And I already showed him where we're going. He doesn't have to be doing this.

I almost give an eager "yes" response, but then I realize he's trying to do what's best for our group, even when it means making things hard for him. What I need to do is the same. I may know where we're going and be familiar with things close by, but he clearly knows these woods better than I do.

"Why don't you continue leading us until we get close and then I can take over?"

His brows lift before he leads us out of the clearing, but there's something different about how he leads that wasn't there yesterday. Something in the way he holds branches out of the way, how he's even more careful helping Annabelle and Tawny, and I let him help me when I need it. Somehow, he's actually very good at being a gentleman. He just needs some final polish on how to treat women.

Is it because yesterday we were running for our lives? We still are today, but without the same urgency driving us. Maybe he can take the time to become even more of a gentleman than he already is?

It takes us several hours to get to the safe house. Hours filled with worry and stress over if we're going to have more problems, but wherever the warlocks searching for us are, it's not here. By the time we arrive at the house, we're all exhausted, too much so to pay any real attention to anything. Not just from the journey but the stress of looking over our shoulders the entire time.

We're safe. For now.

"I'm going to send some messages to friends that can help or may need help," I say.

"Sounds like a good plan," Annabelle says.

I eye Jack, knowing that her statement isn't entirely true, though I suppose I could have done it again without saying anything, but at least he's prepared for it this time. Something in me wants to give him that notice. Probably the something that doesn't want him to take his anger out on me.

I send a note spell to Katherine and then to the last Sanos house I knew Chadwick was going to, hoping he's still there. The note flies off in yellow and dark blue, taking with it my hopes and fears.

It doesn't take long for a different note spell to return. I keep myself from slouching with relief only because the others need to see me be strong. Sometimes, it feels like my strength is the only thing holding things together, but it's not real. I have to fake so much that it can be too weighty.

The note is from Chadwick. Part of me is relieved it's from him, that he's well, but the other part of me can't help but stress about Serena. Why didn't she respond? Why didn't he tell me about where things are with her?

The only thing it does say is that he'll be here as soon as he can.

Does such a short message mean good things or bad? I can't imagine much good taking place now.

CHAPTER 16

There's a restlessness that comes with waiting. Too much time to think on what is happening in the outside world knowing we're not able to do much about it from our small hideout. Cooking, cleaning, and sitting around is all that happens for two days straight. There's a lot of cleaning that needs to be done, which helps. This place has been abandoned for some time. I'm grateful it is here to shelter us, even if it is covered in dirt.

The house is small, two stories with several bedrooms and an attic. The kitchen is large enough to get done what needs to be, but not big enough for more than two people to work in it at a time. The dining room is part of the kitchen, all one big room. When not cleaning, we spend a lot of time there or in the sitting room.

Outside there's nothing but trees, trees, and more trees. This nice little house is far from most civilization. Only a small dirt path shows the way to the main road and it's overgrown. It's one thing I won't fix up.

The cleaning doesn't take nearly as long as I'd like. At the end of day two, everything is in fairly good condition, which means more of just sitting around. I've never been so bored in all my life.

"How can you sit so calmly through this?" I ask Jack, who has been almost meditative through this whole process.

"Easy. Stressing about it won't change anything." He gives a pointed look to my leg that's been jostling up and down whenever I have to sit still.

"It's not like you can just turn stress off."

"You need more breathing exercises," Tawny tells me.

I laugh. "As if I could sit through them."

The laugh doesn't last long though. There's too much pain and worry eating me up inside when there's not a thing we can do about it. We're stuck here with nowhere safe to go and no way to help our loved ones in danger come to safety with us.

"I can't stand this any longer," Annabelle bursts out. "I have to do something. They took my husband. I can't just let them get away with it."

"I feel the same," I say. "Only, what can we do?"

She flops onto the nearest seat, defeat etching her posture. I can't help but think of Zade. Of him being locked up wherever he is. Of what he must be going through. My chest tightens and tears threaten, but I blink them away. Now isn't the time for tears. Crying won't save them, not that I know what will.

"If only there was something we could do. Something that we could make happen. Something to let the Grand Chancellor know we don't approve." I say.

"There is something," Tawny says.

"What crazy scheme are you cooking up?" Jack asks, tone begrudging.

"We should attack back. We don't have to sit and do nothing."

"How do you propose we do something?" I ask wondering how we can accomplish anything.

"We attack a law office. See if we can shut it down. I know it won't get our loved ones back, but it will tell them we are not going to sit by while they do whatever they want."

"It would be dangerous," I say. "I'm in."

All dejection has fled from Annabelle. "I am as well."

"You are all crazy," Jack says. "The only thing that is going to happen is that you're all going to be captured and put in the same position as Councilman Daniel, if they don't tarnish you."

"It's worth the risk," I say. "There's a town not far from here with a law office. It would be the easiest to hit."

Jack crosses his arms and slumps back in his chair.

"But would that put our safe house at risk?" Tawny asks.

"If we do it right, they'd have no reason to suspect this house. And what reason would they have for searching it?"

"Still, I think we should go to the next town over."

"It will mean more walking," I reply. "But we can do it."

"What type of attack spells can we use on a law office?"

CHAPTER 17

I stare at the plain brick building, wondering if we can really do this. It's not like we picked an easy target. Law officers have their position for a reason. If all goes to plan, we won't even be suspected. Which means it had all better go to plan.

Jack glares at us all. I don't know why he even bothered to come, though he said it was because Councilman Daniel would have his head if anything happened to Annabelle. I'm surprised he didn't tie her to a chair instead.

The sun will be coming up in an hour or so. If we're going to do this, we have to do it now.

"Tawny?" I ask. "Are we ready?"

"Ready as we're ever going to be."

Which doesn't feel good enough at all. But Annabelle's right. We have to do something. We can't sit back and let them think they can get away with this. We need to take this fight to them.

I move through the shadows of the buildings until I'm hidden in the darkness right across the street from the law office. My hands go clammy, but I lift them anyway. We have to do this in one swift hit or we'll get caught or end up doing no damage at all, which is entirely unacceptable.

I glance over to see everyone else is in place. Even Jack is helping out, protectively close to Annabelle, hands raised.

Now's the time, but I can't bring myself to say the words. Once we do this, there will be no going back. I'll have attacked someone. A lot of someones. There's even a possibility of people getting hurt. I don't want to hurt anyone. I'm not that type of person. If only there was a more peaceful way to bring this about. But being peaceful about things only resulted in my brother being taken and tortured. We have to do this.

No one else is saying anything. Maybe they're having the same reservations that I am. But we can't let it stop us. We have to move. We have to show our strength. We just have to.

"On the count of three," I whisper. "One. Two." Please don't let this be a mistake. "Three."

I let my power surge out of me. It flows yellow and red next to purples and maroons from the others helping, straight toward the law office. Two spell beams split off to the right, the others to the left. They hit the building with a flash of color and deadly silence.

There's a creak, like the building is cracking, but then nothing. Noise from inside tells me that the law officers know something is going on, but not what. We haven't much time, but I don't want to leave this place without having accomplished something.

"Again," I say. "Now."

I burst out the spell again, letting it tug my magic toward the building and crashing into it. There's nothing. Nothing but the noise growing louder. We can't stay here. We've failed what I wanted so badly to do. What we all wanted. Then all at once, the entire front of the building is crashing to the ground.

Bricks are flying everywhere, dust billowing up.

"Go," Tawny says.

There isn't time to see the rest of the result. We're running, hurrying out of the city as fast as we can. If we can make it out of here, we'll have done the job successfully. There are still the loud sounds of something crashing behind us. I can't believe it worked.

Then, that's not the only sound. People are calling out, footsteps hurrying about. Law officers, most likely. My breathing comes in shallow gasps, heart pounding.

There's still a block of houses to go when we hear the sound of footsteps following us. Jack curses just loud enough for me to hear. I know exactly what he's thinking. We shouldn't have done this.

Maybe he's right. Did I just hurt someone? How much damage did we do? And does this make me too much like them now?

"Over here," a man calls out behind us.

Lands no! "Move it," I say between breaths.

We pick up the pace even more, though who knows how long we can continue like this? A spell flies over head, bright orange. Now they'll have seen where we're at and won't miss a second time.

Tawny shoots several beams of light at them, hitting them to the ground and hopefully blinding the others. But no, they get up off the ground and keep chasing. There's more distance between us now but not nearly enough to save us.

Tawny can't be captured. Neither can Annabelle. These two women mean too much, not only to others but to me. A bright orange spell flies toward Jack. I block it with a burst of green. Too much fear clouding my emotions. No one has to know that except me, though.

I flash a spell back at them, yellow and green, ready to knock them to the ground like Tawny did before. I don't know what else to do, what else will save us. A blue spell zips to me, wrapping around my ankle, knocking me to the ground.

After a stunned moment, I turn and kick at the spell still holding me down. Out of nowhere, Jack appears, slicing into the spell with a green one of his own. As soon as I'm free, I jump to my feet.

"Thank you," I say between huffs.

But we're not safe yet. It doesn't feel like we'll ever be safe again. They are too close, and we are too far from safety.

There's only one thing I can think to do. I picture a barrier between us and them, solid and firm. I thrust the spell out behind us in a wave of dark green. Thankfully the color is dark, glowing in the night, so as not to give us away any further than it has to. Before I face forward, a yellow spell splashes against the shield.

"Faster," Jack demands, like we aren't already going at our fastest pace.

We reach the woods separating us from safety and dart in. Annabelle slows.

"Not yet," Jack says. "Keep going."

She hurries again but says between breaths, "I don't know how long I can."

We dodge through the trees, gasping for breath. A green spell slams into a tree to my right. This wasn't such a good idea after all.

I turn, blasting off another shield spell, putting all my power into it, hoping to give us enough time to run off. There's shouting from behind us, but it grows more distant as we run. And run we do. We go and go and go, everything in me aching, especially my side. I grasp onto it and keep going as fast and as far as I can. The further we get, the more we slow, but we still don't stop. By the time we reach our packs, there's not another sound besides us.

We wait there a moment, and I don't dare believe we actually got away with it. Any moment, the law officers will be back, attacking us again. But no, there's nothing and no one. Somehow, we escaped.

"We did it," Annabelle says.

We sure did something.

CHAPTER 18

The next day, after traveling out of our way to make certain no one's following us, we make it back to the safe house. Everything is as we left it. I can't believe we really did that. We put our things away and go back to stewing over nothing. There's too much time on our hands this way. If something doesn't change, due to boredom, we're going to end up risking our lives by attacking another law office, and maybe this time not be so lucky.

Several hours later, Chadwick strides in the room and, without closing the door, comes straight to me, wrapping his arms tight around me. I can't see anything but his shirt. I can't even move, he's wrapped me so tight. I must make some sort of noise because he lets go with such sudden force, it takes me a moment to catch myself while he's hurrying back several steps.

"Sorry," he says. "I was just worried about you when I knew what happened to Zade in the house you were staying at. I didn't know if..."

"I'm fine. We're fine." I motion to the others, but really I'm thinking about Tawny because she's too close to the line for the Envado throne. Of course, he wouldn't hug someone of her importance like he just did me. Must be why he felt the need to squeeze me extra tight.

"Have you heard anything about Serena or Cynthia? I sent them a warning as soon as I heard, but I haven't heard back from them yet."

"They're safe."

This time, I don't even try to pretend to be strong. I sink into the closest chair, all the pressure built up in me deflating. "Thank all of Envado."

"They have a surprise for you. They will be here soon. In fact I need to return to them and make sure they get here without a problem. I only came to scout it out so I could be sure it was secure and make sure you really were safe."

I'm already on my feet headed toward the door, though it's raining outside. "I'll go with you. We'll be back soon," I tell the others. "Make yourselves comfortable. Cook something if you're hungry. Make yourselves at home here." If any of them even know how to do more than pull out dried meat. "Hopefully, we'll figure something out when I get back."

What is there to figure out, though? I don't know what we can possibly do at this point. At least those I care about here are safe. What I want is to help Zade and Daniel, but storming in to rescue them will end in my own capture, not helping them.

What's more, I haven't any idea where he's being held. Why did things have to get so complicated? Why can't my brother just be safe?

"Of course," Annabelle says. "Take good care of them and yourself."

"I will."

"And I will take good care of the house," Tawny says. And by house, I know she means the household.

"It would be best if you waited here," Jack says.

That doesn't even deserve a reply.

"He's right," Chadwick adds.

I whip open the door and storm out. "They may need help."

Jack glares at me, but Chadwick sighs like he knows there's nothing he can do to stop me. At least one of them has some sense.

I watch for rocks scattered through the forest as the water patters down on us. It's not too far to reach them, only about a ten minute walk in the rain. Only, when I get to them, it's not just Serena, Cynthia, and Lukas, but a couple of warlock guards as well. My girls, all my girls are here. Each and every one of Serena's sisters is here, hovering in a circle with Serena in the middle.

"You're all here," I say as I run to them. "How I missed you all!"

The girls look up at me, relief filling their faces but a tension remaining. They don't seem nearly as happy to see me as I am them. What's going on? Is there some danger I missed? Something more than just the threat of their father?

"Quick, get the girls to the safe house," Serena says.

The guards hurry forward, and with the help of Bethany, Cynthia's next youngest sister, usher forward the youngest girls. Chadwick doesn't waste any time doing as she asked, helping the guard to clear the girls. As they move aside, I realize the problem. Serena's mother is on the ground, hunched over in pain, a stick between her teeth. Sweat drenches her, and the rain makes a mess of her face paint.

She's having her baby, right now, in the middle of the forest. Why could the little one not have waited ten more minutes to enter this world when she was at least in the cabin?

"Don't we have time to take her to the cabin?" I ask.

"There's not time for anything," Serena says.

"I've never helped a birth before."

"Luckily, I have." But her voice says it's anything but lucky. "Do you know any spells that can help with her pain?"

One of the guard stays behind but discreetly looks everywhere but where the action is currently taking place. I wish I could do the same.

I do what I can, zapping a blue spell of calm and pain relief. Pernilla whimpers like it's not enough, but I don't know how to do more. I wasn't trained for this.

It all seems to be over in a matter of moments. Serena takes care of the baby girl while I try and say soothing things to Pernilla. Telling her how beautiful the baby is. How cute, sweet, and pleasant this little girl is. At first Pernilla smiles contentedly, but then her face grows strained. She whimpers again.

"What's going on?" I ask.

"Don't worry," Serena says, handing the baby to me. She's been wrapped in the bottom of Serena's torn skirt. "It's just the after birth. It won't be as bad."

Pernilla lets out a shrill cry.

"That sounds worse."

Serena's forehead furrows. With my free hand, I cast another pain-reducing spell, but I'm afraid it's not enough. If she needed her dress spelled a different color, I'd be so much more helpful. I let her squeeze my hand long past the time it aches while I rock the newest little girl.

"Mother," Serena's voice is uncertain. Scared.

The only response is a groan.

"Serena?" I prompt.

"This isn't the after birth," she says. "She's having twins."

I can't help but give a little smile. There may be too many girls to easily take care of, but I love them all so much. Even this newest sweet one in my arms has stolen my heart. I'm certain we can all make room for a little more love to share.

There's a cry of a new babe that brings a smile to my face. I glance at Serena. She's holding the new baby in her hands, staring down at it as if she's never seen a newborn before. But that clearly isn't the case since I'm holding the twin in my arms.

I take a closer look at the baby and realize why she's frozen. Her plan for another little sister has been exchanged for two siblings. But not just two sisters. For the first time in her life, Serena has a brother.

CHAPTER 19

We do the best we can cleaning up Pernilla and the babies. Serena takes a look at Pernilla's face and gives a sigh, the first sign of emotion I've seen from her since her brother was born. "You're face paint is everywhere."

"I need to fix it," Pernilla says.

"Mother, there really isn't a reason for you to keep wearing it." Pernilla sniffs. "Tradition."

I hand the baby girl to Pernilla while I help Serena clean up. Once finished, I take the baby back. It takes some time, patience, and magic, but we manage to get them back to the safe house. Chadwick and a guard returns and carries Pernilla there.

The whole time, Serena seems to return to her dazed state. Pernilla does as well, but I don't think it's because her newest is a male. She's barely conscious from loss of blood. What is she going to do when she realizes she not only had twins but finally had a boy? That, after all those years of Stephen being angry and punishing her and Serena for all those daughters. And when they finally escape from his reach, he finally gets a son.

If he discovers this, how much more will he try and come after them?

As soon as we enter the door, the girls surround Serena and the baby, all talking at once.

"Two babies!"

"Ah, she's so cute."

"What's her name?"

"And what's hers?"

"Why are they so wrinkly?"

"Can she play soon?"

Serena stares at them, numb. Who can blame her at this point?

"Girls, let's give Serena and the babies some space." It's not my place to correct them. I may be practically family, but practically isn't the same as being real family.

Several groans fill the air, but they quickly all settle themselves around the room, quietly distracting each other. Too quickly and too quietly. What has their father done to them? Has he hexed them since I was away? How I'd like to get my hands on him.

Pernilla is taken to a back room to rest. Serena is still standing, gazing at nothing. I gently go over to her and take the baby from her arms so I have two, one in each arm. "Tawny, why don't you make some chocolate for Serena and her mom?"

She jumps into action, years of being served not enough to stop her from knowing how to make a few basic things. I take the babies back to Pernilla, who is more awake than before. I help them both get settled, not saying a word about the twins or her newest child's gender. Whether that's for the best or not, I don't know. But for now at least, they're all settled.

Then, I finally get Serena alone. The rain has subsided so I take her outside, far enough from the house that we can't be heard but close enough to see it. Serena is a little less pale and has her cup of chocolate in hand, half gone.

"How are you?" I ask her.

"I'm well."

Of course she's not. "Do you want to talk about your newest siblings?"

Serena sips more of her chocolate. "I don't know."

I can't imagine what she must be feeling. It shouldn't matter whether a child is a boy or a girl, but of course, here, it matters too much. And to have two babies to care for on top of everything else going on. I'm about to say something, when she continues.

"It's strange. There hasn't been enough time to have an impact yet. For it to make sense. But I already know one thing." Her expression becomes fierce. "I will do everything in my power to ensure my sister knows her worth and values herself and my brother doesn't grow up to be like my father and every other Chardonian male who only value women as property."

That one little statement packed with such fierceness behind it makes me feel like maybe I have helped do some good. She's not the same girl I came to help a year ago. There's something that isn't just changing here, but has already changed, and for so much the better.

"I'm certain you'll be able to teach him that, and I'll help however you need." I give a wry smile. "I always wanted a little brother to tease."

"Good. He'll need someone to do that. The rest of us are likely to spoil him to bits."

"Oh, I'll do that too." Even though I only held him for a short time, his tiny cheeks are so kissable.

We fall into a silence while I think about how sweet it was holding him in my arms. I never did have a younger sibling, and while there were some babies that Mom took us to visit, there weren't many I spent much time with. There's something so precious about a new little one. No wonder the girls were melting over him, even if they don't know it's a brother.

Brother. It's difficult to even think on mine and what he could be going through right now. I clench my fists.

"Waverly, about Zade..." Serena's thoughts must be taking the same turn mine are.

I wish I had something to offer her. Comfort or hope. I wish I had those things to give myself. But all I have is truth. "We don't know what they've done to him exactly. Or if they are even sticking to the Grand Chancellor's rule about the tournament or if they've gone against it anyway and he's no longer…"

Her expression is stone-like, but her reply is drenched with heartache. "Alive."

The tightening of my throat is so thick and heavy, it's impossible to reply.

"I know it's a possibility. That even thinking about saving him is suicide. But we have to do something. If there's a chance, even a slim chance, we have to think of something. I don't know what to do." She places a hand on her pocket where I know she keeps her gun. "But whatever it is, I'm going to be fighting the entire way."

At this moment, she is so much stronger than me. I want to do the same, but I'm so broken. It's hard to even think about him, let alone plan an escape. "If Zade knew you were risking yourself like that, we'd see the worst of his temper."

"I'd take his temper any time after this." She shrugs. "Besides, he won't know. He's not here."

Right. I want to see his temper again. Want to enjoy his wrath over risking our lives to save him. I can do this. There's time. "Do you think we need to involve Cynthia in this?"

"She'll be furious if we don't. Besides, she's already proven how good at magic she is. We need her if we want even a hope of success."

Even the tiniest bit of hope would be something to cling onto right now. "What about your other sisters? Have you told them?"

Her face crumples with pain. "No. I need to, but I often think they enjoy his company more than mine. They won't take it well."

Not that we are either. It still doesn't even seem real. How can I even tell Mom and Dad? That was the worst thought I could have had. I can't tell them. In Dad's weakened state, the shock and strain of it could kill him. Zade wouldn't even be here if it wasn't for Dad getting sick. The guilt of having Zade come in his place because of falling sick would be even worse. I can't tell them he's been captured.

But if the worst should happen, if Serena and I don't succeed...

"I wish we could keep them from it." It takes me a moment to realize Serena is talking about her sisters and not my parents. "Not to keep them in the dark like women always have been kept, but so they don't have the fear and worry we do."

Exactly. "If only such a world were possible without becoming like the warlocks here. We can send them to Envado where they can at least be safe while we try and rescue Zade."

"And who's to take them? You're the only one I trust that knows the way, but I know I can't ask you to take the time off when it could be spent helping Zade."

And I can't bring myself to offer. "There's Chadwick."

"Please. He's more like a sibling to Zade than I sometimes think you are."

"They don't fight enough for that to be true," I counter. And then I think on all those times I did fight with him. The moments that didn't even matter, but I still got so upset over. Why did I ever yell at him? "I should have never fought with him. What have I done? I may never see him again and that's all he'll remember of me."

"I'm sorry, I didn't mean to upset you. He knows you care, probably more so because you aren't afraid to say what you want to around him and are comfortable teasing him."

It's true, even if guilt is bothering me now. And here she is, comforting me when it's her fiancée that's in danger.

"How did you spring the girls from your father's?" I ask.

She shrugs. "I was going to get them today anyway. It just ended up being good timing with all that's going on. I figured I couldn't leave them there any longer. It was too hard on them. Plus, I thought if Mother had a baby girl..."

I give her shoulder a squeeze, remembering how punishment from their father can get.

"Since father had a council meeting today," she continues, "it was the best chance to help them escape. It was easier than I thought. He didn't even leave any guards."

"Thank goodness the man doesn't know how to protect his most precious possessions. Did you check with all the girls and your mother to make sure they didn't leave anything important behind?"

"I did. It turns out father destroyed all of their things in a fire. Even Mother's. They only had one change of clothes. Nothing else."

"Well, we'll have to fix that the best we can under the circumstances." I want to spit on that horrid man.

"So you think your family needs to stay here for now. Do you think that it is safe?"

"Nothing is safe."

CHAPTER 20

Contrary to how Serena reacted to finding out the baby is a boy, the other girls are all excited to have a brother. They ohh and ahh over him as much as they can. Serena was right. He's going to be a very spoiled boy, though his sister is getting just as much attention. Abigail, or Abby as the girls like to call her, and Benjamin. Ben is a fussy baby but sleeps well, while Abby is a content little girl who doesn't like to sleep at all.

Still, everyone pitches in to help and love the babies. Pernilla, on the other hand, doesn't seem to know how to react to having a boy. She seems numb to it like Serena was at first, only it doesn't seem to want to pass.

A few days pass quietly this way, the girls fawning over the babies and everyone trying to keep up with the chores. Cynthia comes to me after spending a long time talking with Serena.

"Lukas and I are going to try and find out information on Zade and Daniel," she says without any preamble.

"Do you think it's safe?"

"Nothing is safe in this country, but I can't just sit back and do nothing."

That's true, but still. I don't want her in danger if she doesn't have to be. Of course, I also want my brother. "What does Serena think?"

"She wanted to go herself, but I insisted she let me. I have more power and knowledge. I should be able to get in and out of places better than she would. Besides, I've been learning more about the safe houses and people we're working with than she has. I will know where to go to find answers."

"Maybe I should go with you." I'm so torn. I want to be with her, but I've been so busy here helping take care of the girls and Ben. Zade needs me, though. He needs us all if we're to save him.

"If you think it's best, though there's a lot that needs to be done and watching over here. I'd feel better if you were with my family."

My throat tightens. "But Zade is my family. I have to take care of him. I have to save him."

She takes hold of my hand. "I promise we'll do the best anyone can do."

I bite my lip and nod, unable to say anything further. I gather her into a hug. "Stay safe."

"We will."

She and Lukas leave. It's a sad farewell. The days start to pass, slow and agonizing. The longer they're gone, the more I worry. What if something happens to them? What if they're not able to get any news on Zade and Daniel? Or worse, what if they get news but it's bad news? I try not to dwell on it, but it's hard not to.

Chadwick returns with Jack after getting supplies from town. It's easier for Jack to blend in than Chadwick, but neither of them trust the other. I'm not entirely sure what to think of them both now, but at least I trust them with our safety. Jack more than earned that with everything he's done. If he hadn't stopped to cut the spell off my leg, I'd probably be locked up right now.

As I help them put things away, they're both silent and brooding. Something more is going on than they're saying. Not that they're saying anything.

After we finish, I suggest we go outside. Once there, I ask, "What's wrong?"

Jack slumps against a tree.

"We found some people," Chadwick says. "They are hiding from law officers in a forest close to town. They took to Jack, talked to him, and I think they trust him."

"And he wants to bring them here." Jack scowls at Chadwick like he's the most vile thing Jack's ever seen.

"Why is that a bad thing?" I ask, agreeing with the thought to bring them here. What's the point of trying to help people if we don't actually help?

"He doesn't trust them," Chadwick says.

Jack shoots another dirty look at him.

"Well, you don't."

Jack says, "If we let them join us, we're risking everyone here. There's no reason we have to trust that they won't go to the nearest law officer as soon as they know where we are."

"They are hiding from the law just as much as we are," Chadwick counters.

"But they aren't being hunted as much as some of the people here. Turning us in could be seen as a way to make things more lenient for them."

"But they won't because they hate the new laws and won't want to go back to that."

"Yet it's the only life they know. Recognizing their fight against it is useless and invertible."

"That's enough." Both of them look at me as if they forgot I was there. I wonder how long they were arguing over this on the way back. "Look, I know this isn't easy, for any of us, but I think we should consider it."

Chadwick looks triumphant, Jack murderous.

"I think we should ask the others what they think," I continue. "It's their safety in question after all."

"You know they're all going to invite them in despite the dangers." Jack huffs.

"Most likely." Except maybe Pernilla. Despite being numb, she's been over protective, like she's worried that at any moment Stephen will find her and the baby. "But it is their choice to make."

"And I have no say."

"I think you do, just not the only say. You should tell them your concerns because they are very real and valid."

He gives me a look. "I didn't think you'd agree with a warlock like me."

I take a step toward him. "I agree with the truth, which is what you're offering."

"Which is what I've been trying to say," Chadwick says.

I step back. Jack practically growls at Chadwick.

"It would probably help your case, though, if you were a bit calmer and rational." Or a lot. "Trust me, my brother loses his temper a lot and it never goes well for his cause. It has taught me to try to do just the opposite."

Jack gives me a wry sort of smile that sends my feet another step closer to him.

"You do seem like the type of girl to go against whatever someone is angry about just to be contrary," he says.

"At least where the safety of the people I care about is concerned."

He goes somber. "I'm sorry the Grand Chancellor has affected your life this way."

I stare down at the rocks speckling the dirt. "Me, too." I look back up at him. "You do know though, that even if you're calmly talking to them about the risks, they'll probably still want to help those people?"

He shrugs. "It's obvious some people do what they can to help others despite the risks to themselves."

"Maybe the warning will at least help them to be more cautious while they are helping."

"I hope it's enough."

"I do as well." Both him and Chadwick turn to go back into the house. More chores to do, no doubt. There's plenty of them to go around with the amount of people that are here.

"Wait a moment, Jack. Can I speak to you?" When he stops, so does Chadwick. "Alone."

Chadwick shoots Jack a dirty look. "I'll still be close enough you can yell for me if you need to."

I roll my eyes. "You two really need to sort your differences."

"Like that will happen," Chadwick mumbles, but he heads in anyway.

Once he's out of sight, Jack says, "Is there something you needed from me?"

This feels more personal than I should probably get with him, but someone has to look out for him, even if he's a Chardonian warlock. "What you said before, about the others being willing to possibly change things, did you mean that more for them, or for you?"

He squeezes his eyes shut tight. "Just the fact that I'm having this conversation with you should prove I'm willing to consider things changing."

Just consider? It's a step in the right direction at least, and he hasn't told me to lower my head in quite some time. Though he left off in a way that seems like he has more to say. "But..."

"But I'm afraid how I was raised won't change who I am, even if I get a chance to see things differently."

He doesn't give me a chance to think of a response. He hurries back toward the house quicker than he's moved before.

Does that mean he's more a risk to us than even those people who may join us? He doesn't seem to be a threat, not like I thought he was, just lost. What can I do to help him see the way? To see these new thoughts and ideas are good things, not bad? If I can figure it out with him, maybe I can figure it out with others. Maybe Chardonian warlocks are not such a lost cause after all.

CHAPTER 21

Chadwick and I were right. The others do want to help this group trying to avoid the law like us. But they also seem to take Jack's warning seriously. Pernilla is the exception, agreeing entirely with Jack, but with everyone else wanting to help, that's what we're going to do.

We make quick arrangements of how we're going to fit all five them in the house and feed them, for the short term at least. Tawny is the best at arranging things. I suppose living in a castle where there are constant visitors would make her good at that, though here there's not nearly enough room.

While she finishes up, I meander to Jack and Chadwick, who are preparing to go back to the group of people and invite them to come here. I sure hope this is what we should be doing.

"Let me come with," I suggest.

"I don't think that's such a good idea," Chadwick says.

I glare at him.

"You can come if you'd like." Jack's response is so calm and reasonable, I have to wonder if my talk earlier about how you say things made an impact. "But you are clearly an Envadi, and while that's not as bad of a thing as I used to believe, people still fear you."

Not as bad? "Gee, thanks."

"He's probably right," Serena says, joining the conversation. "You know how much I love and respect you, but Envadi used to terrify me. Perhaps I should go instead."

"Zade wouldn't like you risking yourself," Chadwick says.

"Let her go," Jack replies. Maybe the two of them just like to do whatever they can to contradict one another. "People do respect her."

"Chadwick is an Envadi too," I throw out there.

"I'll stay out of sight," he counters.

Men.

"But I really should go," Serena says. "I think they need me to."

She looks more nervous than I have ever seen her before. "You'll be fine," I tell her. "Chadwick and Jack will take good care of you."

She eyes them before pulling me outside where they can't hear us. "That's not what I fear. Of course I don't want anything to happen to me, but if it does, then it does."

"Then what has you so out of sorts?"

"There are people looking up to me. I haven't done anything to make people look up to me. It all just happened."

I place my hand on her arm. "I know, but you're better at this than you think. You've been doing more to lead your sisters than anyone else. Just think of these people as being like your sisters."

She gives me a nod but is pale.

"And if anyone gives you guff," I say, "we can soften them up with a cup of warm milk."

Finally she gives me a smile. "Torture them more like."

"Hey, there's not a thing wrong with warm milk." But I'm glad to see her more like herself.

We both somber back up as I think about the task ahead of her.

"Keep my siblings safe for me," Serena whispers to me.

That's a good reason for me to stay behind. Again. Even though we have a couple of guards, there are a lot of children here. Bethany could use the help. "I will if you promise to keep yourself safe."

"Agreed."

"Don't put yourself in any trouble while we're gone," Jack says as he comes out the front door.

"Or go looking for it," Chadwick adds, following right behind him.

"Go on you three."

As soon as they leave, things are anxious. At least the girls and Ben keep me busy. It's wonderful to reintroduce them to life and how it should be. I only wish they didn't need the reintroduction.

We laugh and play, choosing first a game of tag. Then I teach them a game where one person hides, and the others have to go find that person, joining them in the hiding spot until everyone has found them. Trying to squish into a cupboard with the tiniest girls always results in too much giggling to stay hidden long.

I keep Abigail with me while Bethany keeps little Ben. It makes hiding all the harder when one of them starts to yell. At least it keeps our mind off of things until the girls grow bored of the game. Then it's back to trying to keep everyone happy.

Many hours later, which feel like days, they finally return, a group of strangers with them. Both male and female, though more women than anything else. Most look tattered and rough like they've really been through something. Though their faces are lined with the stress of their situation, they also lighten as they see the house. Until they spot me. Instantly, their guard is up, and none of them say anything.

"Nelly," Annabelle says, going straight to a girl who came in with the group. "How did you come to be here?"

The girl gives me the eye like she doesn't want to say anything while I'm present. "Father said the Grand Chancellor has gone too far, and some of his guards attacked the house. Father and Mother were captured, but I made it out."

"Oh, you dear girl. Let's get you settled somewhere comfortable."

Nelly glares at me again like she could never be comfortable while I'm around, barbarian that I am. I don't want to go. I've earned being here as much as the rest of them. But what's the point? I give up and leave the house, Chadwick trailing after me.

"After all we try to do," I say.

* * *

THE NEXT DAY, while I'm continuing to avoid the newcomers as much as possible, Cynthia returns. They fawn over her like she's a queen, much like I've seen people do to Tawny. To these people, I suppose Cynthia might as well be one. Annabelle's friend must have met her before because Cynthia seems to recognize her and spends extra time talking to her. It takes a while, but eventually, she moves away from the crowd and comes with me outside.

"What news?" I burst out. "Do you know where Zade is?"

"We think he's in the Grand Chancellor's house somewhere. Probably the dungeon."

"The Grand Chancellor has a dungeon? Of course he does. Any news on his condition?"

"None. We just know that both him and Councilman Daniel are there."

I slouch. "At least we know."

She is silent as I try to take it all in. This isn't how things were supposed to be at all. I was going to come here and give Chadwick his message and then, together with Zade, the three of us were going to turn things around. Make Chardonians see how terrible the Grand Chancellor and his ideals are. Make them see how wrong it is to treat women the way they do. Instead, we're in hiding, and Zade is in some horrid dungeon.

The weight on me is heavy. Oh so heavy. "How are we going to break in there?"

"We'll figure something out," she says. "There's one other thing."

"What is it?"

She glances back at the house. "The Grand Chancellor has stopped all trade with other countries."

"What?" Exactly the opposite of what many of the other countries helping us want to happen. I suppose I shouldn't be surprised by it, though, since he's cared less and less what other countries think of him.

"I'm afraid that's not the worst of it." She pinches her fingers together at her sides.

"Just tell me. I can take it."

"He's using the magic from not just tarnished, but servants and lower class women, as a source of electricity."

I think I'm going to be sick. "How could he do that? Why would he do that?"

"I don't know. I just don't know."

CHAPTER 22

Over the next few days, more people continue to trickle in. People who need a place to stay or are outcasts now like us. We take them in and give them a place to stay and chores to do. It takes a lot of work to keep this many people fed and happy. Luckily, the house is stocked for such an event with canned food, but I don't know how long it can last with so many of us eating it.

Only one person comes that I was never expecting. I stare at Phyllis, the girl who betrayed Serena in the hopes of not becoming tarnished herself. Sure, Serena forgave her, and Zade kept her working at his house to keep an eye on her. That doesn't mean I trust her now.

"How did you come to be here?" I ask her.

"There was a group of people I joined. Chadwick came to them with Jack, and I recognized him. I thought this would be a safe place for me." Her eyes are wide like she's scared.

"It will be safe." I move closer to her, for once using my height to intimidate someone. "But that's only if you follow the rules and stay true to us."

"I will," she says. "I swear it."

I let her go with the others, finding places for them all over the cave to settle. At least everyone is willing to pitch in and help. But that doesn't solve the other problem.

"There's too many people here. We're going to get caught," I say.

Jack has a 'no one listened to me' look on his face.

"We can't very well turn them away," Serena says.

"I'm not suggesting that at all. Only, we can't risk everyone's lives even more by continually bringing in people we don't have the means of supporting. Unless we start taking them to other countries, I don't see what other options we have."

"Do you think they'll go?" Lukas asks.

"We can ask at least," I say.

Jack looks like he wants to say something, but it takes him a moment to finally speak. "There's another option."

"Turn them away, we know," Chadwick says. "We've been over this."

Jack grumbles. "I meant something else."

"What is it?" I ask.

"There's this place. It's a little ways away from here, closer to Councilman Daniel's house, or his previous house now. There's a hidden cave, but it's giant and has fresh water. We would still need to figure a way to get food for them. And it would probably still be a good idea to take those out of the country that can and want to go. But the cave would be better than this at least."

No one speaks as we all absorb the new information. If this had been when we first met, I would have suspected him of trying to get us captured. But Annabelle's old house probably isn't being carefully watched like it was before. There'd be enough room to slowly sneak people there, I think. Besides, if these people want to stay in Chardonia, none of our safe houses are big enough. We have to give this a try.

"That could work," I say.

"It just could," Chadwick reluctantly agrees.

"Would you take me there?" I ask Jack. "We can look over

options and make certain it's ready. And that it hasn't been found by the Grand Chancellor's men."

"Of course."

"No point in waiting. Let's go."

While we are gone, the others plan to talk to everyone about staying in Chardonia or leaving to another country. Whether or not this cave will work, changes have to be made, and soon. At the rate we're going, we'll be found by the Grand Chancellor's people very easily.

We walk through the forest for quite a while. I'm on edge the entire time, worrying about if someone else is out here. If we'll get caught. But we make it without a problem.

The cave is close to the lake by Annabelle's house. The house itself isn't visible, which is fortunate for us. The entry to the cave is covered by a bush, but once inside, it's a huge network of caves, big ones and small ones.

"I think this should work. I only worry that we're going to be too close to a house that has been taken over by those against us," I say.

"We will need to be careful about that, but they won't be expecting us to be here either," he says.

Like what I was thinking of before. "Thank you for showing this to me, Jack."

"It was nothing."

"No, I mean it. You didn't have to do any of this. I know you've been reluctant about everything we've done, but I want you to know I'm very grateful for all you're doing to try and help us."

"You're welcome." The tone of his voice makes me think more progress is happening than I thought.

* * *

OVER THE NEXT WEEK, we move everyone to the cave. I make certain Serena's family has a little cavern with lots of space so they have plenty of room to roam about, though Ben's cries can be heard just about anywhere in the system of caves.

I also help with some newcomers, one of which is a Chardonian man who's been helping us since before I joined the group aiding Chardonians. Theodore, a man with a bushy beard, brings not only a few people with him but some desperately needed food.

At this point, I'm starting to wonder how many people are going to be left in the country to do the Grand Chancellor's work. I try not to think on him too much, though. It makes me livid.

The people flock to Cynthia and Serena. While they may be famous, Tawny and I are to be avoided like condemned warlocks even though we're anything but. Each encounter is worse than the last. Still, I try. How else will they know I mean them well if I don't keep trying? This particular morning is a tedious one.

One woman is struggling to get all her things in the cave along with her seven children.

I hurry over to her. "Here, let me help."

As I near her youngest daughter, perhaps five years of age, she screams, a blood curdling sound that chills my very bones, and throws herself on the ground away from me.

"What did you do to her?" the mother shrieks at me. "Get away."

Nelly rushes over, picking the young girl up and whispering in her ear.

Heat flames my cheeks, wishing I wasn't so tall and distinguishable as an Envadi. "I was just trying to help."

"You can help by disappearing," the mother yells.

Very well, then. I hurry outside. What was I thinking, trying to help a people that still thinks I'm a barbarian? Why can't they see that it's the Grand Chancellor that's the barbarian? That all I'm trying to do is help?

Tawny walks out of the cave and comes straight toward me. "The people are just trying to get used to us still."

And how much more will we have to do for them before they are used to us? "Maybe. But I think the people would be happier without me."

"They're just still getting accustomed to having both an Envadi and a woman be as strong yet caring as you are."

"As we are." For she's just as strong, if not stronger than I am. She just knows how to make her strength apparent in the background of things while I run headlong into idiocy. How am I supposed to get them accustomed to it? It's not as if we have time. Every day Zade and Daniel are gone from us is another day their lives are in jeopardy.

CHAPTER 23

A few days after everyone is settled and assigned their tasks, I take Cynthia and Chadwick to try to get more information on Zade and Daniel. And if possible, to help them escape. That's what I really want. What I ache for. I miss my brother more than I thought possible. And it is an excuse to get me away from people who hate the sight of me.

I don't tell Serena or Annabelle how badly I want to be able to help them escape, only that we'd get her more information. They both take it so bravely, but it's easy to tell by the look in their eyes they're both hurting.

I always thought Zade's property and house were huge, but even in the dark, the Grand Chancellor's makes Zade's look like a playhouse for children. There are at least four floors with towers at each corner, all of it made of some type of white stone.

Not only is it huge, but it's lit up like a load of fireworks. To think he's doing that with lower class women and warlocks who owe debts makes me want to go hex all his lights out.

It's disgusting. Even the Queen doesn't have so much property, and she has the staff living with her, plus half of court. How does one person become so obsessed with themselves?

"How could we get in?" I whisper.

"To that lit up monstrosity?" Cynthia says, "Who knows. It might be better to go during the day with how bright it is."

"But then we have to fight the lights of day as well," I say.

"And it's likely guarded with spells and not just people," Chadwick adds. "Especially the dungeon. Just look at the colors we can see and think of all that we can't see."

"Just standing here is making me nervous," Cynthia says.

"What do you think, Bethany?" I ask.

"There's someone coming," is her reply.

We all bunch down further, hiding in the forest close to his property.

"Who is it?" Cynthia whispers.

"Quiet," Chadwick replies.

Whoever it is, is coming closer. No, not just closer, straight for us. Do we hex whoever it is or do we run? There's nowhere to run to. Anything we do will get us caught. I reach out my hand to send a hex his way.

"Wait." Bethany yanks my hand down. "It's Nathaniel."

"What?" I ask.

"The Grand Chancellor's son."

I knew that, but knowing it and having it make sense are two different things. Despite knowing that he's one of the people that stuck up for Serena, I still want to hex him. He may have been spelled to take those women's magic from before the tournament, but I still remember what it did to Cynthia. Watching her almost crushed under his power. A power he still carries.

I put my hand back up, but Bethany pulls it back and whispers, "You guys stay down."

Then she does the stupidest thing ever. She stands.

"Bethany," Nathaniel exclaims. "What are you doing here?"

"Just thought I'd look around the area."

"You have to go. It's not safe."

I stand. "Why not?"

"Shesh. How many of you are there?"

Like I'm going to admit that. Before Bethany can answer, I say, "Enough."

He glances at me out of the corner of his eye and then turns back to Bethany. "There's very little time before they will come out as well. You're here for Zade and Daniel, aren't you?"

Bethany and I give each other a look. I say, "What if we are?"

"You can't break them out. The spells my Father has guarding this place are too intense for even an army."

I want to collapse to the ground. That can't be it. "There has to be something we can do."

"Not that I know of right now, but I promise you I will do what I can to help you."

"You will?" Bethany's voice is so hopeful, but I have my doubts.

"How?"

"I don't know yet, but we'll figure something out. If there's somewhere I can meet you in two days, we'll have time to discuss things then."

Is this a trap? "I don't know."

Serena jumps up, "We'll do it."

"Good. There's a big rock about a mile east of here in the forest. Meet me there."

"How'd you know we were here?" Bethany says.

"You're not the first people to try and break someone out of here, you know. Father put me on guard duty after the way everything turned out at the tournament."

"Lucky us," Bethany says.

"You guys have to go. Now."

"We'll see you soon."

I drag Bethany with me as Serena takes off. The boys follow behind us, seemingly not worried about showing their presence now. As soon as we're out of danger, I ask Bethany, "How do you know Nathaniel?"

"I've talked with him at Serena's ball and several times at the tournament."

"Must have been some good talks if you already trust him so much."

She shrugs. "Sometimes you just know when a person is trustworthy."

* * *

I DON'T SAY anything when we return to our hideout. Neither do Cynthia or Chadwick. But Serena goes straight to Annabelle. Neither is seen for the rest of the evening.

CHAPTER 24

W e wait for Nathaniel at the rock he told us about. It's bigger than I am so it's not easily missed. We're early of course. We're all too anxious to be anything but. I just hope that he really isn't turning us in. Of course, if he were doing that, he could have gone ahead and done that two days ago when we were at his house. Bethany seems to trust him. That will have to be enough.

There's a crinkling of leaves. I put my hands up, ready to hex whoever it is if it turns out to be a trap. It's just him. I put my hands down, though they tingle to stay up and on guard.

"You made it," Bethany says.

"Of course."

"What can you tell us? How are Zade and Daniel?" I practically shout.

His mouth tightens. "They're alive."

Part of me is instantly relieved, but the other part of me fears where this is going.

"Yet..." Serena says, voice trepid.

He shakes his head. "The most important thing is that they're alive. Father isn't kind at all, but they're both strong, and I'm doing what I can without Father becoming suspicious."

Bethany puts a hand on his arm. "We appreciate that."

"Do you speak with them?" Serena says.

"Not often."

"Next time you do, if you can, would you tell them we love them?" Her voice is so small, but my heart feels even smaller.

"There's a spell around them to keep track of everything they say." At my gasp, he continues, "Don't worry, I warned them about it. I can write messages down to show to them, but only if no one else is around. I will try my best to get the message to Daniel and Zade. It would raise their spirits."

Mine, though, feel lowered. There's a lot he's not telling us. At least Zade is alive. For now, that will have to be enough.

"What can you tell us about the Grand Chancellor's plans?" I ask.

"What do you know?"

We spend several minutes exchanging information on what we do know. On how the Grand Chancellor brought both Chancellor Ryan back and made Stephen a Chancellor. How he's using people as a power source. And on how he plans on using the tournament as a big display of power. All things we already knew.

"That's as much as I know," Nathaniel says.

I can't help but feel blue at this. Don't know what I was expecting but something more. Anything.

"So there's nothing you can do," Serena says, sounding more bitter than I've ever heard her before.

"Now, not as much as I'd like," he responds. "But I want him out of power as much as you do. He's an evil, vile man. We'll keep in contact, and I'll gather as much information as I can."

"Then we'll have to hope you stay safe while finding something useful for us," Bethany says.

We exchange information on the next time to meet. And though we know a little more than we did before, I can't help but think of Zade locked in the Grand Chancellor's basement going through things so horrid, Nathaniel wouldn't even speak of them.

* * *

THERE'S no telling if we can rescue Zade and the others or not. After everything we've tried, it feels hopeless. We didn't even come close, and all we gained for our trouble was almost getting caught. It's not just Zade and the others' failed rescue that's the problem, but there's so many people here that now want change, yet nothing is happening.

As time goes on, things feel even more hopeless. We can't come up with any new plan to save Zade and Daniel. The longer they're imprisoned, the more I lose faith we'll ever save them. And what must they be going through? I don't want to even imagine.

What's more, our hidden group grows and grows every day. We can't stay hidden for long. There's one thing I notice, though.

Where are all the tarnished?

These people had to come from homes with servants, places where tarnished were needed. Not all of them had tarnished, I'm sure of it. Annabelle had a few herself. So where are they all now? Don't they need help as well? Or has the Grand Chancellor managed to capture them all? Most of them do have those tracking spells that are now mandatory for all of them. I have to talk to Katherine. To find out what's happening with them as well.

I send her a spelled note, hoping it reaches her. I miss her sorely and worry over her. How is she surviving without Zade to help hide her? If she would answer my notes and meet me in person, I'd be able to help at least a little. Though without having insight into exactly what Chancellor Ryan is having their tattoos spelled what color next, it's much more difficult to ascertain how to help. There has to be something I can do, though. If only she would contact me.

After all this time in the cave, there hasn't been much of a chance to talk. Cynthia, Serena, and I go out to pick berries. Or really, to talk without being overheard. The cave isn't the most private of places to talk. The morning is deceptively bright for the chill in the air. Still, I manage to talk about a lot until I finally overload on my frustration of this war.

"We're all doing as much as we can to influence them for good, to get them to see more in life, but I don't know. There's no telling if our efforts will make a difference." I voice my frustration to Serena and Cynthia.

"It's true," Cynthia says. "It feels like fighting against a wall spell, except I don't know how to break through it."

Serena says, "Things have to change. Warlocks have to change. Women have to change. The new system has to change. And they're already doing so. The Grand Chancellor needs to feel the consequences of what he's turned this society into. I will do whatever it takes to help bring these people down. Even if I have to use a spell to do it."

My spirits lift with each word she says. I've never been more proud of the journey she's made more than at this moment. "I guess it's time to see if we can get those who've come to us to help do something about it."

"I think you're right," Cynthia says.

It will be a big job, though, one I'm not sure we can do despite all of Serena's strong words. But we have to at least try.

"They will come around," Cynthia says. "I know they will."

"They do seem to trust you two," I say. And Jack. They trust him the most out of everyone. "I think we need to have Jack be a part of this. They trust him."

Cynthia and Serena both agree. Serena's mouth tightens, and she blinks rapidly.

"What is it?" Cynthia says.

"This isn't just about trying to help those who've come here. As good as that is, there's something that may not be as big as trying to change a whole society's perspective, but still something important. Someone important."

"I want him back, too." She sniffs, and my own eyes tear in response, but I don't let them flow out. "We'll just have to hope he can last through whatever it is they're putting him through, that he can make through it until we can figure a way to save him. Because we will save him."

Though I don't mention that the possibility of him still being sane is slim. Even if he is still sane, how scarred will he be? Will he be so damaged he won't want anything anymore? She knows this, probably even better than I do. My brother, who he was, is most likely gone from us forever.

CHAPTER 25

As I sit in the kitchen with little Ben strapped to me with a length of cloth, I tell myself I can do this. I've asked for help before. This is no different.

Who am I kidding? It's totally different. Asking for help for something small like organizing a ball or learning a new spell is entirely different than asking about overthrowing the most powerful man in the country.

No matter. Whether hard or not, it needs to be done, and Jack is the one who's become most like a leader in the short time our group has been together. If I want to convince them, he is the key. Too bad we got off on such a horrid start. Things have been better between us, though. Just not sure if better is good enough to convince him this is a good idea or not. It will all depend on how much he's really changed.

When I find him, he's shelling peas, so I sit next to him and help without saying a word. Ben, for once, stays nice and asleep as I assist. It's an activity I usually find relaxing, but nothing is relaxing about it today.

How does one bring up how they want to start a rebellion?

Zade would be so much better at this than I. Or Chadwick for that matter. Maybe if I had joined their lessons on how to be a good spy I would be too. So much for all the frivolous things I learned. Who cares about pretty nails? I can't even remember the last time I spelled mine.

"Is there something you wanted?" Jack snips.

"Why would you say that?"

"Never before have you worked in the kitchen with me without being asked. Plus you keep scrunching your eyebrows together, making this tiny line between them."

I suppose I am being really weird. "Can we go for a walk?"

Phyllis gives me the eye. No matter. Their thoughts don't matter yet, only Jack's. If I can get his, the rest will come. Hopefully.

"Something serious?"

"Isn't everything serious here?"

His eyebrows twitch as if to say touché. After putting down the peas and cleaning up the shells, he says to the others, "We'll be back in a while."

I follow him through the maze of caves out into to the open where the fresh air brightens everything.

"So, what is it?" he asks.

Despite the change of scenery and lack of eavesdroppers, I can't bring myself to just say it. But there is something else I can say. That I need to say. "I'm sorry about how things started with us."

"That's what this is about?"

I round on him, Ben stirring as I do so, hands fisted on my hips. "You can't even be nice when I'm trying to apologize. What is your problem?"

He does the strangest thing, at least for him. He smiles. "Forgive me. I didn't mean to sound so brash. It just didn't match my expectations of what you wanted."

"Oh, well." I drop my arms to my sides. "What were you expecting?"

"That you wanted something. I don't know what, but some type of favor from me."

Only a favor valued in lives. "There is something."

He smirks.

"No need to look like that," I say. "It wasn't too hard to figure."

The smirk leaves, replaced with an expression I can't read. "No, it wasn't hard to decipher at all. You though, you are much more difficult to discern."

Something lovely flutters through me. "Only if you try and read too much into things."

"It's how I was raised. To be aware of everything and what it means. To become a councilman."

"You were being groomed to be a councilman?" With his attitude when I met him, I shouldn't be surprised, but with his station, it seems like a lofty goal.

"I know what you're thinking. I am—was a servant. How could I be a councilman? It wasn't always this way, though. Several years ago, my father was wealthy and about to become wealthier," he says. "But things change."

"How did they change?"

"My father got deeply in debt. Councilman Daniel found me and said I could work for him and he'd treat me fairly. His offer was the most generous I received."

Daniel and Annabelle are most giving. "What happened to your father?"

Jack shrugs. "The mighty has fallen."

"He's working off his debt as well?" I guess. Ben stirs so I begin rocking back and forth to calm him.

A nod is the only response I get.

"This isn't where I meant our chat to go." I sigh. "Look, I'm sorry. Even though I've spent a lot of time in Chardonia now, I'm still not used to the way men treat women. You've proven over the last while that you aren't like the others." Though I'm still not sure that means, he's ready to help us gain freedom. "I just wanted you to understand there was a different way to do things. I shouldn't have lashed out at you."

"Apology accepted. Though I must apologize as well. I'm still learning how to properly treat women. I'm not sure I know anymore."

Wow. "You're definitely headed in the right direction."

He gives me a tentative smile, which I return.

"So, about this favor…" Jitters come back in full force.

"Yes?"

Just time to spit it out. "We would like help overthrowing the council."

His eyes widen briefly before his calm demeanor returns. "You don't ask for small favors."

I want to say something sarcastic, but things are just too heavy to add that in. So instead, I say nothing at all.

"This is because of your brother."

My chest is heavy at the mere mention of him. Truth isn't what I want to go for but probably will work best. "Yes, but not wholly."

"Explain."

"The world I grew up in was so different. Women are not only respected as people, but they are allowed and encouraged to pursue their desires. Whether through magic, part of government, or business. Even if they want to be a wife and mother, the position is revered not as a means to getting warlock babies and girls with magic worth selling off. I've been here a while. It's not just hard to see how women are treated here. It's wrong."

He crosses his arms and leans back slightly. "You realize it goes against everything I was always taught?"

"Just because you were taught it your whole life makes your way right?"

He stares off in the distance without a word.

"Maybe it doesn't matter what someone has been taught their

whole life. Maybe it's right or maybe it's wrong. Maybe the only way to know for certain is to trust your instincts."

"I'll think on it."

Not the answer I wanted, but at least it's not a no. "Fair enough."

CHAPTER 26

While we wait for Jack to decide, I take matters into my own hands, helping the others to prepare even if they don't know it yet. Of course, it's something they should learn no matter what's to come. Magic.

The men here already know it and have even put up with Cynthia and a little bit of Bethany casting spells, though not so much me. That will have to change, though, because the women need to learn to harness their powers.

"Would you like to help me teach anyone interested how to do magic?" I ask Bethany.

"Wouldn't Cynthia be a better choice?"

"Better, no. She would be helpful, though, but she already has so many responsibilities, I can't see adding one more to her list."

"True. It would be nice to have an excuse to take a break from my little sisters."

Poor girl has been spending almost all her time with them, trying to teach them and keep them entertained. The sister next in line after Bethany should be able to assist. "I'm sure we could find others willing to help. Presha can do a great job with them. Go ahead and spread the word. We'll start teaching tomorrow."

And we do. At first, there aren't many girls that show up. A couple ladies who are old enough to be mothers. One woman who is old enough to be a grandmother, and several who are younger than me. At first, they're all timid about trying, but soon they're all into it, their grins growing bigger with each casting of a spell. The spells are brightly colored, ranging from simple spells that are straight colors, to harder spells that move things around.

Not only that, but they gather a crowd around them. Each time we practice, the crowd grows a little bigger. A few more women join us in practicing, but most still only watch. At least they're taking it all in. The only thing that is not good about the situation is that most still try to avoid me. I know why, and I even understand it. But that doesn't mean I have to like it. At least they're learning.

* * *

TWO DAYS LATER, there's finally a meeting with Jack. He stands across from me, arms folded. "You, Serena, Cynthia, Annabelle, Nelly and, well, all lot of the women here, working with them every day. Helping them survive. I've learned things from them. Things that I never would have learned otherwise."

Wow. That's more than I expected from him. At least so soon.

"I've thought on your request to help."

When he says nothing further, I prompt, "Did you come to a decision?"

"I believe I have."

"What do I need to do to find out the answer?"

He grunts. "You have to understand this isn't easy for me."

"Is that a good sign or a bad one?"

"Depends on your perspective."

"You're maddening."

Jack raises an eyebrow at me with a grin and then sombers. "I…I had a sister."

Had? And what does this have to do with his decision? "Were you close?"

He laughs, but it's tainted with a deep bitterness. "No. She avoided me as much as she could. Which she should have. I was cruel. Teased her, hexed her. Then she was tested and sold off to an old warlock. It was supposed to be a good thing for our family, a raise in status and wealth, but..." He shakes his head.

He continues, "It doesn't matter now. The point is, I thought it was the correct way to act, treating her as such. I thought it was the way things were supposed to be. My friends all treated women that way. When I'd help with a training for class, they'd encourage the same. My father, well, he wasn't always the harshest warlock, but women were definitely objects to him."

His description leaves a bitter taste in my mouth. This doesn't sound like the talk someone gives before accepting to help you overthrow other men who act the same way, even if he did preface it with how helping women has changed him.

"Yet, now my sister has been gone years. Shortly after that, I came to work for Councilman Daniel to help with Father's debt. Things were different there. I've never seen a warlock treat a woman the way he treats his wife. And he's kinder to the other women as well. It's stuck with me. Made me think on how I treated my elder sister. How she always avoided me, yet adoration shone in her eyes when she looked at mother. I felt like I was missing something. And then you. You came along."

"And probably ruined any kind thoughts you had about women with how incredibly harsh I was."

"You were harsh." But he smiles, a real genuine smile that makes my stomach flutter. "But it was the first time I've seen a woman be so, well, warlock-like. Confident. You never lower your face to a warlock. You don't even mind talking to one like there isn't any consequences to your words. You are nothing like Chardonian women."

"Thank the queen for that." And does that mean he sees me as a positive thing? "But I'm hoping more Chardonian women can gain that confidence. They are people. They have rights. They need to know it."

"I'm beginning to think you're right."

Did he really just say that? Jack? The servant who's been mean to me and apparently his older sister? "That you think so gives me hope other warlocks may feel the same someday."

"It also means," he takes a deep breath and lets it out in a puff, "yes, I will help you. Though it will probably mean death to us all."

My mouth would hang open if my mother hadn't drilled into me to keep it closed. "I don't know what to say. I admit that's not the answer I was expecting."

"Yet it is what I've been leaning toward with everything I've been doing."

"Yes, it is. Forgive me. I've been thinking that you aren't as strong as you really are. I've gotten to know you better than that, seen how loyal you can be. I shouldn't have judged you so harshly."

"I did bring it on myself."

"Maybe. But maybe my preconceived ideas need to be unlearned as much as yours."

"That might be true." He gives a half smile. "I will help, and I will give everything I have."

"Thank you."

But he's right. This may very well mean death to us all.

CHAPTER 27

"You do understand that I can't make the others want to participate in our suicidal rebellion," Jack says.

I try not to let his words deflate me. "You have more power over them than you think."

"I have less power over them than you think. The only reason they're letting me lead them is I'm the only warlock who's stepped forward to do so. If another warlock came along and started punishing them, my position would be done for."

"Do you really think they would? They're finding freedom to speak in here, to play and to walk around without an escort. They're finding a life without hexes and beatings. They're already seeing how much better life can be without that."

"I want to hope otherwise, but I think it's so."

Exactly the type of thing I'll keep working on. "We'll just have to do the best we can then."

"About that…"

A sudden influx of trepidation fills me. "What?"

"As much as I don't think I can influence them much since I won't punish or hex them, you have even less influence than I," he says. "Truthfully, I believe that anything you support they will actively work against."

This is beyond ridiculous. Sometimes I am so through with this county. "Because I am a woman."

"You are. And an Envadi woman at that. Two terrifying counts against you as far as they're concerned."

Well past done with this country's backward ideas. "I thought we had grown past this."

"Perhaps some, but they are frightened. After years of abuse, they've been chased from their homes. Some, like Annabelle, had a warlock who treated them better, yet they still understand how brutal the world is against women. And they all have been brought up to fear Envadi ways. They won't want to become a barbarian like you very easily."

These people have such twisted views of what barbaric is. "Still, they have accepted Serena and Cynthia."

"Not as leaders, or at least what they think of as a leader. Those girls are guiding these people, but they're doing so in their own subtle ways. Slowly teaching and instructing. You're...more straightforward than that. You speak exactly what's on your mind."

"And an Envadi."

"There's that as well."

Why does he have to keep bringing that up like it's a bad thing? "Do you think I'm a barbarian as well?"

"I think..."

"Go on. You've said enough already that more isn't going to hurt my feelings."

He grins, so soft and slowly, it's hard to watch anything except it. "You are so stubborn."

"I try," I say. "And you are trying to avoid my question."

"Fine, then. You're not at all barbaric. But you are not only stubborn but brash. And beautiful." What did he just say? "Also, you're strangely quirky. Warm milk? That's only for people on farms that are desperate. Not people who have access to things like an ice box."

"Have you tried it?" Even though that's what I said, my thoughts are still on the fact he called me beautiful. The room is growing hotter.

"I don't need to."

"You haven't. I knew it. Tonight we're going to change that."

"We don't have to."

"Of course we do." I stare him down, and he stares right back. I'd keep it going and win because I'm just that stubborn, only I think of something more important and soften my gaze. "Thank you for doing all this. For putting up with me and helping us out. We couldn't do this without you. I couldn't do it without you."

He leans a little closer. "You're welcome."

Warmth floods through me, a nice kind of heat, but somehow it leaves me uncertain. "I'm going to go get that milk heating," I say before I hurry off.

It's good that he's helping. We really need him too. But that's not where my thoughts really want to go. They want to linger on him, and the warmth I felt from simply being closer to him.

CHAPTER 28

The biggest cavern in our network of caves is full of people we've found. My hands are shaking as I look at them all.

"Are you certain you are ready to do this?" Jack asks.

Serena to my right, Cynthia to my left, and Jack on the other side of us all as the group gathers. Tawny is waiting at the back of the crowd with Annabelle, supporting us as best they can from there. If I were alone, I'd say no. If it'd been a year ago, I'd say no. If I listened to common sense, I'd say no. But I've passed all those things and am ready to follow what I know is right regardless of how hard it's going to be.

"Let's do this."

"I suppose it's time, then," he says.

We're silent as our group of survivors gathers together. We're such a small group. It seems like there's more of us when it's time to eat, but there's really few compared to how many are in the entire country. There's not even enough here to start a real rebellion. Not really. Yet as they crowd into the main cavern, it seems as if there's many of us gathered together.

My palms grow sweaty. I discreetly pat them on my pants. If Annabelle and Cynthia can wear them, so can I. Of course, with

Annabelle everyone thinks it's endearing. With Cynthia, they think it's fitting her station since doing magic at the tournament and winning. With me, well, I'm just the barbaric one. The crazy one. And they're all about to think I'm even crazier.

Jack and I decided if we're going to go through with this, we might as well be honest about the fact I'm involved. Hopefully Serena, Cynthia, and him are enough to dissuade any negative impact I may have. I can't lie to them, though. They've been through too much of that already.

Once they're all here, Jack says, "We've all been together for a while now. Gotten to know each other a little. I'd like to think things are different here than what you're used to."

Several heads in the crowd nod in agreement.

"To that end, I believe we can be honest with each other." He pauses, in which all my hopes seem to teeter on a cliff. "You've all gained a little more freedom here, albeit a cautious sort of freedom that comes with hiding from the law. I've discussed some of this new freedom and different attitudes with these ladies, and we think, we believe, there is a better way of living."

"What are you saying?" someone from the crowd calls out.

"I'm saying, we should make this our way of life without interference from those now leading us," Jack says. "I'm saying we should try to overthrow the Grand Chancellor."

As one, those gathered gasp. And my hopes jump off the cliff, soaring somewhere unknown. I can only hope they land in a better place than they began.

"This isn't just your idea, though," Theodore says.

"No, as I said, it is something I've discussed with Serena, Waverly, and the tournament winner, Cynthia."

"We already know how you feel," someone else calls out. "We've seen how you act, Jack. You're a leader like a man should be. These ideas are mostly from them. That Envadi bringing her strange ideas here."

"Why should we follow *her*?"

Whether it's wise to speak up or not I say, "Because it will lead to a better life for everyone. Don't you want more out of life? More freedom? More happiness?"

"You're an Envadi. You're probably just here trying to get us to overtake our government so we'll be an easy target for your people to come in and rule us."

"Haven't you seen what Chancellor Zade was doing before they captured him? Haven't you seen how he's helped?" I say.

"And haven't you all seen how Waverly has tried to help us? She's worked harder than anyone else here," Cynthia says.

"It could all be a ruse," another says. "A trick to make us think she's helping, but as soon as we let her in, they're going to take over our lives. Make us all like the tarnished to support them."

"They want to take away the little that we have gained," Phyllis says.

"They want to help," Tawny calls from the back.

"I understand your fears and reservations," Jack says. "Only a short time ago, I was questioning the same ones. Yet after thinking on it, I believe these women are correct. We need to do this. We need to fight against this. Though we don't have warm homes and food readily available, haven't you enjoyed the freedom we've found not living under the Grand Chancellor's constant threat? Even having to hide from them, fearing they may discover us at any time is better than being told you have to be tarnished or a slave for those greedy slobs."

The crowd is silent now and no longer restless. His words are having an impact on them, making a difference. More than he thought they would.

"What if we did want to overthrow the Grand Chancellor? Then what?" Theodore asks.

"Then we would do it," Jack says.

The crowd begins to murmur amongst themselves. I bite my lip, hoping against all hope that they understand how much this is really needed. How they are the ones that need it. And how much I wish I could say more. How I wish they would trust me to help them.

"I'd be willing to try," a woman calls out.

"And so would I," says a man.

Soon, the whole room is full of affirmations that people want to do this. We are going to do this. Together. Whether wise or not, we are taking on the Grand Chancellor.

* * *

AFTER THE MEETING is over and the crowd disperses, I say to Jack, "Thank you. We wouldn't have been able to convince them to help if it wasn't for you."

"I only used your words to convince them. Perhaps after some time they will grow to understand how much you're trying to assist them. How good you really are."

Heat floods me. "I'm just trying my best." I clear my throat. "Now that we have the people on board, what do we do?"

"This was your plan. I thought you knew."

I suppose I should have thought about that better. "Train them I suppose. And we have contact with Nathaniel. He should be able to give us some insights on where would be good places to attack." I hope. If he doesn't have the information now, maybe he'll be able to get it for us. "That's what we need to work up to fighting them. Somehow taking them out."

"There's truly not another woman like you." He shifts his weight. "It's a good start. I'll see if we can get some of the warlocks in place on the outside. Ones who are the most all right with this plan and won't give under pressure. See what information they can collect for us. Between the two plans, I believe we'll be able to make some progress."

"*If* we can get the people to cooperate."

"We'll be able to do it."

"It'd be easier if they didn't hate me so much."

"They just don't know you yet. Look at us. We fought when we first knew each other, and now we're planning a rebellion together. Give it some time."

"Time is the one thing Zade and Daniel don't have."

CHAPTER 29

While we have tried to include others when teaching the girls magic, not many have wanted to participate. Now that they have agreed to help us overthrow the Grand Chancellor, this changes drastically. Almost all of them want to learn, save for a few stragglers, the ones most disinclined to our plan. Cynthia takes over most of the teaching, but Bethany and I continue with Serena and Jack's help. Tawny also helps but in a more subtle way. She guides those teaching, giving them new spells to learn.

None of the women know how to fight, whether with magic or not. A few of the warlocks know how to cast magic, but only the simplest of spells. Of course, that's because most of the stronger spell casters have been recruited for the Grand Chancellor, whether be it as an 'elected' council member or a law officer, or some other person he can keep a close eye on and influence.

But it doesn't matter if we all still have a lot to learn. It doesn't matter if most have done nothing but cower under others' commands. It's those reasons that will make them strong. Those reasons that will give them the will to fight and win an enemy who has held them back for so long.

The only question I have now is whether my presence here is weakening them instead of strengthening them.

When they watch me doing spells easily, they chatter amongst themselves and stare a lot. So I keep casting spells, even when I grow tired and my magic low.

"She seems to know what she's doing," one says to Serena.

Finally. Progress. I throw out a spell that Tawny taught me last night. A bright, flashy spell that's nothing more than fuchsia coloring, followed by an almost clear spell, tinted only a little red by my emotions. The red tinted spell slips around the side. Just as the fuchsia spell bursts, the other spell stabs into the target, leaving a gaping hole all the way through the target as it burns its way through.

Phyllis comes up to me. "Do you think you could teach me that?"

"I'd be happy to." Not happy, thrilled, ecstatic, over the moon.

As she lets me teach her, it's a nice change, but she still doesn't want to get close to me. Every time I step a polite distance toward her, she steps back three steps. She doesn't want to contaminate herself with being too near me most likely.

"The first part is easy," I say, giving up on being close enough to really help her. I feel like I have to yell for her to hear me. "It's just using your pure magic. Throwing one strong emotion into it, and picturing it bursting in front of your target. Using it as the distraction."

She doesn't respond, but her eyes narrow at the target. It takes her a moment before a spell comes out, bursting almost as soon as it leaves her hand. A few of the bystanders swear at the bright flash of yellow.

I blink, trying to get my sight back. "That was good. You just need to focus it out farther so you can blind your opponent instead of yourself and your teammates."

Her only reply is to scoff. I guess she doesn't mind blinding me so much, though I'd think she'd at least care about blinding herself.

"Why don't you give it another go?" I say.

She shrugs her shoulders and puts her hand up. I want to close my eyes, but I force myself to keep them open. This time, she's successful; the yellow light is tinted with orange but shoots straight for the target, a dummy in the shape of a human made from bags and straw. Once it gets there, it bursts just like it should. She tries three more times, and the burst gets bigger every time.

"That's right," I tell her as she finally gets the spell down. "You've got it perfect."

She shrugs again.

"Now let's work on the second part of the spell."

She steps back from me. "Actually, I think I'm done."

From the tone of her voice, it sounds more like she's done with me than with learning a spell. She turns her back toward me and walks away without a word. Swell. My thoughts are confirmed when she leaves me to go directly to Cynthia. I guess I can't hope for too much in one day. It doesn't make it any easier to deal with, though.

CHAPTER 30

Jack, Bethany, and Serena join together in what's become mine and Cynthia's room, a small cavern furnished only with bedding and our clothes. It isn't the best of accommodations, but it gives us some sense of privacy. Plus it gives me a chance to voice my thoughts yet again. Though quietly so someone can't hear me through the echo.

"It's time to move to something real," I say. "We've got to strike them where it counts, and we need to do it now."

"Agreed," Cynthia says.

"We do need to attack where it will hurt them, but with the least danger to us," Jack says.

Always so reasonable. I want to huff at him, but how can I? These people have entrusted their lives to us. Not just now, but in the future as well. What's the point of fighting if we get most of them killed? I would rather die myself than have any one else do so.

"I have an idea," I reply, hoping it's actually a feasible one. "What if we attacked one of the power plants and rescued all the people they're taking advantage of? Not only would they be losing power, but those people need to be freed."

Cynthia says. "And they'd likely want to help us if we're the ones that freed them."

"But would they be guarded by men and spells?" Jack asks. "There's no point in risking our lives if it's as heavily guarded as the Grand Chancellor's."

"I can ask Nathaniel what he knows," Bethany says.

She's always so quiet. I almost forget she's there. "Let's do that. And in the meantime, we can keep training them. It's going to take more than just the handful of us if we want to make a real difference."

"I have another thought," Cynthia says. "We can attack Chancellor Ryan's house."

"We'd need to ask Nathaniel about that as well," I reply. "I don't know if he'll be able to get that information or not."

"No need. I already staked it out," Cynthia says.

"You did not," I practically shout. "You could have been killed."

"Lukas was with me."

I glare at him and then roll my eyes. No point in getting upset over something that already happened. At least it wasn't Tawny so carelessly risking her neck. If her mother found out all she's doing, she'd have my head. Then again, the Queen may have known how dangerous it was here. Maybe she wanted Tawny to come and have the experience to help her be a better Queen when it's her time.

But my thoughts are trailing off. I need to think on the here and now. On Cynthia at Chancellor Ryan's house. "And you found what?"

"It's only guarded with spells. They appear tough, but once you take a closer look at them, they're easy to break through," she says and grins. "Ryan is overconfident."

"Let's start there, then," Jack says. "While Bethany learns more information about the power plants, we'll attack the Chancellor's home. That will be the perfect place to hit first. Who'd like to head up the task?"

"I believe I'd love the job," Cynthia says.

"I'll go with." Someone needs to help Lukas keep an eye on her revenge so it doesn't get out of hand. But oh the joy this will bring. Our first real hit, right to the second in command.

CHAPTER 31

J ack insisted on coming as well. So there are four of us
hidden in a crop of trees, staring at a house surrounded by
all sorts of flashy colored spells. It looks like a rainbow
dome threw up over the entire house.

"Are you sure this is just flashy?" I ask Cynthia in a whisper.

"Not only is it just flashy, only servants are home. Ryan is with
the Grand Chancellor."

I shake my head, trying to be hopeful, but I have to be honest
with myself. I'm more scared than I've ever been in my entire life.

We move closer to the building, waiting a little each time we
move. When we stop, Cynthia concentrates a moment before
sending out a spell, each one unraveling a little more of the throw
up rainbow dome, getting us a layer closer to the house. She was
right, the spells are fierce looking, but for her, they're nothing to
break through.

When we're almost to the mansion, an animal starts howling.
Grand. A watchdog.

"You didn't say anything about a dog," I tell Cynthia.

"I didn't know there was one."

We sit tight for several minutes, but the dog never comes into sight. All the while worry flutters through me. If we're caught before were ready, it could mean a fight we don't want. But the way remains clear. "I think it's safe."

Jack nods and, together, the four of us make our way closer still. Suddenly, there's a bang of a door closing. We dive to the ground, practically eating the grass that used to be under our feet. My heart thuds in my chest.

Through the line of bushes, I see several warlocks headed our way. Stupid dogs.

One warlock with a deep voice calls out, "Who's there?"

Might as well get this over with. I give Cynthia a glance. She nods.

Together, Cynthia and I rise, standing together. My full height usually leaves me feeling odd in Chardonia, but not tonight. Tonight, its full effect has me towering over these bumbling servant idiots, powerful and strong.

"It's a barbarian and the witch," one of them squeaks.

They want me to be a barbarian? A barbarian I'll be.

I run straight at them with a warrior scream. At the same time, Cynthia zaps a black spell streaked with crimson at them. They cower like frightened Chardonian women before scampering away.

As soon as they're out of earshot, I turn to Cynthia laughing. "We should do that again."

"Definitely." She's laughing as well.

Jack stands, and he is most definitely not laughing. "Don't worry. There's going to be more chances for that than you want."

That sobers me right up, even if it was funny to see the looks on their faces.

We move toward the house, not another guard in sight. I suppose the throw up dome was supposed to deter everyone. The building is massive. Four floors and as wide as Zade's. Who knows how many people could be hiding in there?

As we stand in front of the main door, I say, "I feel like we should knock."

"It does feel that way," Cynthia says.

Jack shakes his head and barges forward, swinging the door open. A butler stands several feet away.

"Get out of here if you don't want to be hexed," Jack growls.

The butler scampers off. We hurry through the halls, searching the house, servants running from us as Cynthia flashes spells at them. We gather what supplies we can carry in our packs, food that's much needed. "It's too bad we can't take more of this with us."

"There isn't time," Jack says. "They're sure to have warned Ryan, and we can't be slowed down."

I sigh as we leave the house, packs full. It's just a shame not only to waste all this precious food but to destroy such a beautiful building. We stand out in front of the grass, and I suddenly worry that we've missed someone in the house. It was so big, and we moved through it so quickly.

I can't worry about that too hard. This is war. We were kind enough to go through the house before hand.

"Do it," I tell Cynthia before I chicken out.

She faces the building, and with a spell of flaming orange and yellow, she sets the building alight. It quickly blazes up, bright and hot. If there is someone left in there, I hope they have time to escape out the back. For now though, we've done what we came to do.

We run then until we're far from the building but can still see its glow in the distance. We are armed and dangerous now. Message sent.

CHAPTER 32

With more confidence now that we had a victory, we can press forward with more hope. Only there's still such a long ways to go. To try not to stress about it, I join Tawny in helping to teach others, mostly girls, about magic. She's smiling and laughing with them, comfortable with helping, even if they aren't as comfortable with her.

"Good morning," she says as I join them. "Have anything fun to teach us today?"

"Just the usual."

Some of the girls groan.

"Come on," Tawny says. "Show us something fun. Did you girls know that Waverly is one of the most talented Envadi at spelling dresses and getting people ready for balls? Her talent is extraordinary."

"Show us something," Nelly says.

The other girls immediately start clamoring for something fun as well. It's not helpful at all in terms of learning to fight, but I suppose it is a lot of fun. Besides, if it gets them excited about magic and practicing it, all the better. And they aren't cowering from me.

I spend the morning teaching them different spells, starting with a simple nail color changing spell and working up to adding sparkles to clothes and face paint. They ooh and ahh over it, all making me wish I'd thought of the idea sooner.

When I finish, I say. "This is war. We can't only change the color of our dresses."

"I wish we could make it that way," one of the younger girls says.

Me too. But there's more spells to teach them, useful spells like a shield spell that could save their lives. And food that needs to be gathered and people that need to be settled into places to sleep, and chores that need to be done. There's just so much. So many people that need help, and I'm only one person. There's not enough that I can do.

"How about this," I say. "For every three attack or defense skills you learn, we'll learn one fun spell."

"I like this idea," Tawny says. "I'm sure there's lots you can all learn that way. Sometimes learning the fun spells can help make you better at the necessary skills anyway. Practice, you know."

Phyllis, who's been lingering on the edges, says, "How much can we really learn anyway? We're just women."

"Don't you remember that spell I taught you before?" I say. "The one where you made a burst of light?"

"Yes," she grudgingly replies.

"If you can do that, you can do so much more. As women, we have more strength than we know." If only I could get them to believe that and to believe in me.

* * *

AFTER THE OTHER girls have gone to bed for the night, I turn to Tawny. "Do you know any healing spells?"

"Quite a few. They're required in my schooling."

I wish they'd been required in mine. "Would you teach them to me?"

"Of course. Is there any particular reason you want to learn?"

"With all this fighting, people get hurt. I hate feeling helpless. I want to be able to do something if it's needed."

"Good enough reason for me." She claps her hands together. "Where should we start?"

"With whatever's easiest."

"How about with whatever's the most useful?" She gives me a sly grin.

"It's going to be hard, isn't it?"

"Whatever gives you that idea?"

"The look on your face."

She laughs. "Maybe you'll have a better aptitude for it than I do."

"One can only hope," I mutter under my breath, hoping that I can pick it up easily. There isn't a lot of extra time around here to be learning new spells. I'm too busy helping with the girls and Ben, chores, or teaching others to do magic.

"It would help if we had an injury to work on." She gives me a look.

"Oh no, I'm not injuring myself just to fix myself."

"Fine. I will." Before I can stop her, she pulls out a spell that leaves a cut on her arm.

"Tawny," I yell at her, "you can't be doing things like that to yourself."

She shrugs. "It's for a good cause. Besides, look at it. It's barely a scratch."

Indeed, it is the tiniest of scratches, just enough to draw blood. "Maybe," I grudgingly admit, "but don't do it again. We can find other ways to practice."

"I suppose you're right. There has to be someone around here that's hurt themselves."

"Exactly. Now, how do I fix it so I don't have to feel guilty about you hurting yourself for me any longer?"

"Like any other spell. Picture your magic stopping the flow of blood and knitting the skin together."

"Just like that?" I ask, skeptical that it would be so easy.

"Just like that."

Which I know should be true, but having never done this before, I'm more worried about making it worse for her than making it better. Still, I have to try. I need to be good at this so I can help when real injuries happen. For they will, no matter how hard I try to stop them. That much is already apparent.

I picture the flow of blood stopping and her skin covering up the wound. Once it's in my mind's eye clearly enough, I call on my magic to do exactly that. The spell comes out white, tinted with green. It moves to the cut, quickly stopping the flow and healing the skin back together. I'm a little tired by the time I pull my magic back in, but not by much.

"Well done," she says. "It took me more than a dozen tries before I could even get the blood to stop flowing. You're a natural."

"It's about time I'm a natural at something." Relief that I can do this, that I will do this and help people, fills me. Now I only hope that I don't have to use it.

CHAPTER 33

As encouraging as teaching the women and girls to fight is, there are other things to worry about. Things not nearly as enjoyable. Despite what food we gathered from Ryan's, we desperately need more, but the amount of warlocks we have with us is being heavily outweighed by women. We need warlocks to go out with women so they don't get in trouble with the law officers. Though there's no promises that that will help. Most of the warlocks who have come to us have been placed back into society where they can do more to help us from the outside. That's the hope anyway.

With such a limited number of warlocks though, and with such a great need, we decide to have one warlock with two women go search for food. I'm placed in a group with a guard I'm unfamiliar with and Nelly. The entire walk to town, she stays as far from me as possible, despite our strides forward yesterday.

How am I ever going to get these people to trust me? It's frustrating being here to help and being treated like I'm the enemy. It eats at me, gnawing at my concentration.

Suddenly, there's a law officer in front of us. Dandy.

"What are you doing here?" he demands.

"Just going for a walk," our guard answers.

Not a good enough excuse at all. Not for the first time, I wish I could do more in this country.

The law officer circles us both, stopping in front of me. "Going for a walk, huh? With what appears to be an Envadi scum."

I tense, my muscles bunching, though ready to run or fight, I'm not sure yet.

He grips my chin and forces my face down to his. "Are you an Envadi scum? Or just a freak who looks like one?"

I don't answer that. What good answer is there? Instead, I twitch my hand toward him, ready to zap him with a hex should it prove necessary.

He lets me go and moves to Nelly. "And what are you? A freakishly short Envadi?"

"Leave them alone," the guard says.

"Are you going to make me, Envadi lover?"

Our guard's hands are clenched into fists, but he doesn't prod the law officer further.

The law officer chuckles. "That's what I thought. Now, let's take you in. Walk toward town, and don't try anything funny. I'll be following you."

We can't go to the law office. If we do, the only reason we'll come out again is to be tarnished or buried. Our guard looks over at me. I nod my head to the law officer. Suddenly the guard whirls on the law officer, flashing him with a yellow hex.

The law officer screams with rage, zapping a midnight-blue spell at our guard. The guard falls to the ground. The law officer puts his hand up toward Nelly.

I race toward the warlock, throwing a fireball of anger straight for him. He must sense it coming because at the last moment, he throws an icy-blue shield up protecting him for the blast.

Nelly screams. Great way to call more attention to our situation.

"Run and get help," I yell at her.

The warlock blasts an orange spell at her, but I block it. He glares at her like he wants to capture her, but he knows I'm the bigger threat. One of the leaders who have led so many people to hide from their vicious ways. A barbarian at that. He zaps a cutting spell at me, slicing into my stomach.

I fling a fuchsia spell at him that sprays him with sparkles. Gee, why don't I just decorate him to death? He sends a black-tinged blue spell my way. It looks deadly in its shine. I throw a bright purple wall up. The blue spell smashes into it, followed by two more of the same thing. My shield spell weakens, draining my power.

Help had better arrive soon. I don't know how long I can hold him off. An orange hex bashes into me, searing my left arm and chest. I groan in pain even as I fling back a sliver cutting spell. He blocks it with a wall of green, but lets his guard down too fast. I zap a sleep spell at him in a soft blue that's deceiving in its quickness.

It slams into him, but not before he has the chance to throw out one last spell. I try to bring up a shield spell, but too late. The gray tinged aqua spell pounds into my already searing chest. I drop to the ground, light-headed.

I can't pass out now. I force myself to crawl. Each move agonizing as I near the law officer. When I finally get there, it's all I can do to see he's knocked out. I fall to the ground.

Faint voices call my name. Someone puts their hand on my shoulder while probing my wound. I open my eyes, but I can't make sense of the scene. Jack is above me, but his eyes are withered with worry.

"Hold on. Help is coming," he says. "Just hold on."

"Is she safe?"

My words are faint, even to my own ears, but he replies, "She's safe and well. You'll be well soon, too. Please hold on."

My eyelids flutter closed. His slightly scratchy cheek rubs

against mine as he whispers in my ear, but the words no longer have meaning. The nearness of him is calming. Relaxing. The world goes dark.

CHAPTER 34

Something smells familiar. Warm and comforting. But also kind of aggravating. Like I need to defend myself from a fight. From hostility. The mixture of feelings is so confusing. And I hurt. My stomach like it met brutal punishment. I must groan or make a noise because a male voice says, "You're fine now, I've got you."

Instead of feeling fine, I feel riled up. I just can't remember or think of why. What happened?

Finally, I force my eyes open. Jack is cradling me on his lap. I jolt up. Or try to anyway, but I collapse back down with a grown as my head pounds and chest aches. "Ow."

"Don't get up yet. You're still not fully recovered."

As the memory of the fight, the memory of almost losing Nelly returns, I groan again. She may not like me, but I don't want to see her hurt. Of course, now I'm the one in pain. Those girls need to get better at casting spells.

He brushes his finger across my head. "Take it easy."

"What happened after I blacked out?"

"We brought you here. Cynthia will return soon to assess how you're progressing."

"That doesn't explain why you're holding me."

He looks away and surprises me by, instead of letting go, tightening his grip. "I was worried about you."

"You were worried about me?" My pounding head makes it harder for the words to make sense. "In what world does that make any sense?"

"It doesn't."

"At least we can be in agreement about something." Even if it doesn't make sense, there's still something there. Something more than just pain. The way he's touching me, holding me close yet softly like he doesn't want to make my injuries worse. Something about it is undeniably right.

Cynthia clears her throat. "May I look at your injury?"

I realize Jack and I have been gazing at each other. I blush and look at her. "Go ahead. Is it serious?"

"No. I would have fully finished healing it already, but I don't have the full skill to know how."

The spells she uses is soothing, cooling the irritated burn on my stomach.

Once she's finished healing me, she asks, "There are some people who would like to talk to you. Can I let them in, or would you like some more time to recover?"

"No. I'm fine now."

Her eyes flicker to Jack, and I realize I'm still lying across his lap and in his arms. I try to sit up, but my stomach is still sore. He gently lifts me, though I'm uncertain how he manages without hurting me more, and places me on the bed.

"May I be of service in some way?" he asks.

Lands. This is really different. "Um...no, thank you. I'm well."

"I'll leave you for your visitors, then." And with that, he leaves the room.

Cynthia hurries over to me, adjusting the blankets around me. "What was that?"

"I was hoping you'd have some idea. Was he with me the entire time?"

She nods. "He was the one that brought you in. Refused to leave your side even while I healed you."

"I knew we'd been less hostile toward each other lately, but this…" This is something more than I ever expected. Something nicer than expected.

Cynthia's tucking abruptly stops, and she sits on the bed next to me. "You like him."

"I think I do." And what dreadful timing for it. We're in a civil war.

There's the scrapping of someone walking toward our room.

"Several people have been anxious to see you. Must be one of them, but I can send them away if you're not ready?"

"No, it's fine."

She nods, glances over me once to make sure I'm comfortable, and motions for the person to come in. Chadwick steps in.

Chadwick. Jack. Zade. The men in my life are becoming all too complicated.

CHAPTER 35

C hadwick, fortunately, doesn't stay long, only long enough to determine that I really am as well as Cynthia said I was. The entire time, I'm remembering how it felt to be held by Jack and trying not to feel guilty because of it. Chadwick knows there's nothing between us. But I know he still hopes that will change. That the path everyone in Envado thinks we are going to take is the one we are actually going to go down, to become engaged. I used to think it could be, but now?

After Chadwick's hurried departure, the next to come visit me leaves me feeling as if I got zapped by another cutting spell. Why can't I soften the guilt I have surrounding me?

There's another sound of someone walking to the small cavern. Cynthia rounds the corner, speaking softly. "What do you want?"

The reply is too quiet to hear.

"You will be nice or you will be forced to leave. She's healing." She moves out of the way to reveal Nelly.

I may have saved her life, and wanted to do so, but I'm not sure I want to see her right now when I'm already in pain. It hurts enough physically. I don't need to hurt emotionally as well.

Nelly takes the chair Cynthia had been sitting in while she leans against the wall, her presence somehow soothing while I don't know what's to come. How is one supposed to feel after saving someone's life?

A more awkward silence than I've ever been a part of follows. What's the point of all this? To torture me more with her presence? Or is there something more?

When I can't take it anymore, I say, "Is there something you needed?" So it came out a little harsher than I meant. I did just have my stomach ripped open.

"I..." She seems to steel herself, for what I can't be sure. Not after the way she's treated me, even if I did just help her. "I wanted to say thank you for saving my life."

Another silence follows as I try to digest what she said. What she means. Before I can form a reply, she continues.

"And that I'm sorry. For everything. The way I've treated you, especially. You haven't deserved any of it. All my life I've been looked down upon because I'm a woman, and I despised it. Yet I've looked down on you just because you're an Envadi."

"It does seem a little backward," I say, not knowing how else to respond. A thank you I might have guessed at, but an outright apology? The incident must have scared her worse than I first thought.

"So maybe we can be friends now?"

This just keeps getting a weirder. "Yeah, maybe."

"I really like how you spell your nails. Do you think you could teach me how to do that?"

I grin at her. "Now we're talking."

We spend another ten minutes talking about different spells and things I can teach her and the things we have in common. It's more than I expected, but it helps that she has always hated being suppressed. She seems to want freedom any way she can get it. By the time she leaves, I feel like I finally may have found a way to connect with another Chardonian woman.

166

* * *

NELLY WASN'T the only woman whose opinion of me changed. All week visitors come, some saying nothing, others talking on and on about life in the cave. But a few actually apologize to me for being so rude. I've never heard anything like it in all my life. Who knew all it would take to get people to respect me and be kind was to almost die?

CHAPTER 36

Thanks to magic and time, I heal almost fully in the matter of a few days. I'm still sore, my stomach aching whenever I move, but I've never let a little thing like that stop me. Especially not when things are dire enough that someone almost died.

I gather the core group of leaders together, determined to set things in the right direction. If we don't do so now, we'll wax strong in misery and defeat. I look them all over: Jack, Tawny, Serena, Cynthia, Bethany, Theodore, Annabelle, and Chadwick. It's quite a group we've got going, but is it enough for what I think we should do next?

"This is not good," I say. "We can't have them bringing the fight to us and then barely surviving."

"I'm not sure they are strong enough to take the fight to the Grand Chancellor yet," Cynthia says.

"Are they ever going to be?"

"Eventually."

"Zade doesn't have time for eventually," Serena shouts.

We all look at her. Raising her voice is so rare. The pain of having Zade gone is finally getting to her.

"Sorry," she says.

I give her a hug. "There's no reason to be sorry. I agree with you completely. We can't continue to do nothing."

"If we're not strong enough to attack the Grand Chancellor, but we can't wait, what are we possibly going to do?" Theodore asks.

"What do you suggest?" Jack says to me.

"While we wait for the others to get stronger and learn more, it's up to us to stop the Grand Chancellor and his men from making any more progress. It's time to take the war to them. Bethany brought news that could help." I turn to her.

"Nathaniel has discovered a power plant that's not well guarded. It's far from any town so they don't think anyone knows about it or would bother to try something with it."

"That's the one we need to hit, then," Cynthia says.

But Bethany doesn't look so sure.

"What's the problem?" I ask her.

"Just the location," Bethany says. "It's one of the few areas in Chardonia that's not forested and it's flat."

Lovely.

"We attack at night then," Cynthia says, her enthusiasm never waning.

If I was as powerful as she is and accomplished such feats, I'd be just as enthusiastic. Though, in my defense, I did help at Ryan's and to save Nelly. I can do this too, no matter how fearful it makes me.

"With a bigger team than last time," I say. "Not too many, but some we can trust."

"What happens if we all go and the worst happens?" Tawny says.

"Some of us should stay behind," Chadwick says, giving her a pointed look.

"Definitely," I say. "Tawny would be a good choice. And Annabelle, if that's all right?" I can't have something happen to her and have her husband lose her before we save him. Serena should stay behind as well, but knowing her stubbornness, I'm not going to be the one to bring it up.

"I'm fine with that. I think the people here are growing fond of me."

"I'll stay with her," Theodore says.

"Bethany?" I ask, unsure which side of this she wants to be on.

Her lips pinch. "I want to go. I really do, but I think I should stay behind this time."

"Jack?"

"I'm going, of course."

His response surprises me. I thought he'd want to stay behind and protect Annabelle. I'm glad he's going to be with us, though. "That's great. We will put a group together, then. We head out for the attack in a week."

CHAPTER 37

Katherine's finally come! She's walking straight toward me with a male tarnished at her side. He looks to be just a year or two older than her, and his tattoos don't glow at all. Her tattoos glow deep red, the color they were when Zade was captured. She must not go anywhere public with the wrong color. The law officers would take her as soon as they saw her.

I wrap her in a hug. "I've missed you so much. It's so good to finally see you."

"Even better to see you."

I release her. "Who is your friend? I don't believe we've been introduced."

"This is Charles. We are... that is to say, we were going to be married."

"Married! I didn't even know you were serious about anyone." I shake Charles's hand as he steps forward. "You had better take excellent care of her."

"Wouldn't dream of doing anything else."

Suddenly, I turn back to Katherine. "Wait, you said were. Why were?"

She clenches her jaw before a neutral expression takes over. "There's too much going on right now. What with the rebellion, Zade being captured, and people being taken and killed. Not to mention there's no one who we could find to perform the ceremony."

"Oh, Katherine." I wrap her in another hug. "I swear sometimes this is the stupidest place on the entire planet. I'm done with all these Chardonians getting in the way of important things, especially love."

She gives a half grin. "I knew you'd understand. Where's Serena? She's met Charles before but didn't really get a chance to know him. And then we can talk about how we can help with the rebellion you're taking part in."

"I'm so happy you're here!" I start toward the cave opening. "Serena's inside, probably with someone that has all sorts of concerns and wants her to fix them."

"She's changed since I first met her."

"You're telling me."

The view darkens as we enter the cave.

"What's a tarnished doing here?" someone calls out.

Lands. I finally get their trust in me, and we're going to have to go through it all again with Katherine. She'd better not have to almost die for someone to earn her trust. "She's here to help."

"How can a tarnished possibly help?"

"This tarnished can do more things with clothes than you could ever think of."

"Clothes? Truly? We're supposed to be happy about something less than a shadow to help us with a bunch of silly clothes?"

Heat boils in me, but before I can snap a reply, Katherine puts a hand on my arm. She gives them a withering look. "I can camouflage you so you can hide in a forest or get close to a house or party. I can make slots for you to easily carry weapons. I can disguise you so you look like you fit with any group, including the upper class. I can keep you alive with a bunch of silly clothes."

I want to tell her how majorly impressed I am but not in front of everyone

Those gathered aren't so easily swayed, though. It's enough that the hassling stops, but they still keep a close eye on her, watching her every move. I hurry to get her out of sight, toward the cavern Serena is staying in.

"Sorry," I tell Katherine. "They're very mistrustful."

"I know what you went through to gain their trust. Ridiculous rumors. I had been hoping they'd be more open to me since I'm a Chardonian woman just like many of them, just like Serena and Cynthia. Seems it was wrong to hope."

"Give them time. They should come around without anything drastic having to happen. You're much less abrasive and blunt than I am. People like you."

She bites her lip. "Maybe, yet there's too many things dependent on a good relationship here. If they can't trust me, I can't give them my full help."

"I wish we could change it faster for you," I say.

"Posh. For now, I'll still help how I can without interfering too much. I'll send clothes at least." She turns to Serena. "And this whole debacle has turned me rude. Serena, do you remember Charles?"

She smiles. "I do, yes."

"We are trying to find a way to be married."

Serena squeals with delight. We spend the next hour lost in a world of love and weddings. Only, no matter how long we're distracted, there's still the real world out there waiting to destroy us.

* * *

ONCE SHE'S had a chance to talk with everyone she wanted to, I bring Katherine to my room to chat. I wish Jack was here to introduce her to, but he's away getting more food. It's just as well.

There's much to discuss without introducing her to a man I'm not certain how I feel toward exactly.

"How have things really been?"

"It's been difficult not being able to go anywhere in public. My whole store was broken into. A warlock stole all of my clothes, material, and designs—after which he destroyed the shop."

"Oh, Katherine." I give her a hug. "I'm so sorry. These warlocks are going to get what's coming to them. I'll make sure of that."

"I have no doubt you would show them exactly how you feel about it."

I guess I'm not very good at hiding my spells or my feelings. "Can I unspell your tattoos to no longer glow?" I ask her.

"You can try. A few others have tried and haven't been able to take the color out."

"Let me see what I can do." Though hearing others have tried and haven't gotten anywhere with it is discouraging.

I try to study the spell, see what exactly it's doing. It appears simple enough, just light glowing from her tattoos. There has to be more to it, though. I know there's some sort of tracking system related to it, but she shouldn't have that piece. Not with Zade taking care of it for her.

I focus in on the colors, taking them out, and cast the spell. The spell is clear except for some light gray streaks. It moves over her face in light waves, covering the redness glowing from her tattoos. The redness seems to fade under the spell, and my hopes rise. I pull the spell back only to have my hopes dashed again. They are as red as ever.

"I'm sorry," I say. "I thought I had them."

"Don't worry about it."

"Wait, maybe Tawny can do it. She's dealt with invasive spells before."

"I'm willing to try anything at this point."

I hurry to get Tawny, who wants to try. Serena comes over to chat with Katherine by the time Tawny and I return.

"No promises," Tawny says. "But I will do my best."

Tawny takes her time studying the spell. While she tries to discover how to counter the spell, I glance at Serena. She is twisting her hands but otherwise appears calm. Why is she so stressed about this? Even if Tawny can't counter the spell, Katherine has been living with this for a long time. Things will be all right. Unless, of course Katherine, isn't the problem. It's Tawny. I should have never brought her here, given not only how volatile things are, but also how rough her being here is on Serena.

I move to Serena and give her a quick squeeze, letting her know I'm there for her. We wait a few more moments, and Tawny finally tries her counter-spell. It's clearer than mine was, with just some faint yellow sparks. It focuses in on Katherine's tattoos, covering them all. Just like my spell did, the red fades as the spell covers over them. Unlike mine, it stays faded when the spell pulls back.

"You did it," I say.

"Really?" Katherine reaches up to touch her face. "They're really gone."

"Let me run and grab a mirror," Serena says.

She returns quickly with a small mirror in tow. I don't bother telling her we could have spelled one easily enough. She may have accepted magic, and even wants to learn it, but she can't seem to remember how much it can really help in everyday life.

Serena holds up the mirror, and Katherine's entire face transforms, lighting up with joy at the sight of her unglowing face. If only it was so easy to get rid of her tattoos so she didn't have to continue life as a tarnished.

"Thank you," Katherine tells Tawny.

"Of course."

"Maybe at some point, I'll let my hair grow out."

"What color is it?" I ask.

"Dark brown. I haven't missed it, though, other than when I'm cold."

Chardonia feels cold to me, at least in my heart. I hope we're changing that.

CHAPTER 38

The time to attack the power plant has come, and I'm not at all ready for it. I don't even know what to expect this dark night. Katherine made us all a fabric drape to go over our clothes that looks like camouflage. It helps us blend in even though there's no forest to hide in. The building up ahead doesn't look sinister. Not at all like I'd expect one to look like that's using people for their magic to power a mad man's dreams.

It's plain brick with one wooden door in the front. The only thing odd about it besides the wires coming out of it is the lack of windows. I can't imagine staying in a place with no sunlight streaming in.

"Is everyone in position?" Jack asks. He's such a natural leader. I can't imagine anyone else taking his place except maybe Chadwick. But of course the Chardonians are ever stubborn. They may have become more accepting toward us, but that doesn't mean they're ready to let us lead. No matter, as long as we can help.

When Jack gets affirmations all around, he motions for us to head out. From here on, there won't be any talking unless absolutely necessary.

The first spell we come to is like a simple brick wall. It's like even red rectangles with white lined between them, only this wall is transparent. Cynthia hits it with a dark gray spell, plunging a hole big enough that the ten of us can get through.

Chadwick takes our rear while Jack and Cynthia head us up. They get through three more spells similar to the first, the last one leaving Cynthia panting. But there's no more spells between us and the building.

I motion Cynthia to take my spot while I watch Jack's back. The door of the building is unguarded. Probably due to a mixture of having the spells guarding it and being too far out here. Jack motions all of us to move flat against the wall. As soon as we're all hiding, as best we can, Jack knocks on the door.

Several moments later, a burly warlock with a stench I can smell all the way over where I'm at, answers.

"You my replacement?"

"Yes, I am."

"It's about time you got here. Get in here."

"Of course. Sorry about being late." Behind his back, Jack slams one fist on the other, indicating one of us should take this guy out.

I cast a sleep spell, knocking him to the floor. We hesitate a moment, just long enough to see if anyone is coming. When no one does, Cynthia strengthens the spell for him to sleep even more, and we drag him across the ground to the other side of the building out of sight. He's so heavy, it takes all of us pulling and shoving to get him there. The fact that he sleeps through it all is a good sign.

"I'm going to go through first," Jack whispers. "If this warlock mistook me for his replacement, perhaps the others will as well."

I nod. If only we knew how many others there are for certain. We don't know exactly what we're walking into.

Jack heads in first. As the rest of us wait outside, I can't help but imagine a plethora of horrid things that could happen to him.

What if he never comes back? What if I never see him again? What if he's badly injured? Or worse?

I shake my head in the direction of the door. Chadwick firmly shakes his head and holds up two fingers, indicating we should wait two more minutes. Which maybe we should, but what if he's in there being hexed to death? Waiting is only going to make that worse.

Each second of those two minutes is torture, to stand there and do nothing. When they're finally up, I reach for the doorknob.

"Give him another minute," Chadwick whispers.

I shake my head, but before I can turn the knob, the door bursts open.

I jump back, but it's only Jack.

He gives me a small grin but tainted with something I fear. "There's no other guards in here. That guy was the only one."

"Don't tell me that means we need to drag him inside," I say.

"Let's leave him out here." He gives me a look. "I think it might be best if you girls stay out here."

"I don't think so," I retort.

"What she said," Cynthia adds.

"It's up to you," Jack says. "But it's not a pleasant sight in there."

A chill grips me, pricking my whole body with its iciness. "We can't help if we can't see it."

Lukas takes a hold of Cynthia's hand. The action makes me want to hold someone's hand as well. But whose would it be? Chadwick or Jack? Why are either of them even on that list? Chadwick is what's expected of me, and Jack is—now isn't the time to think about this.

Jack leads us in the building. At first it's nothing more than a hallway. Nothing on the walls, just fresh white paint and bright lights on the ceiling. Too bright. Glaring.

We walk into a big, open room, the middle of which is a bright purple spell around some sort of machine that goes up into the ceiling. I don't spend much time trying to figure it out, though, because of what's surrounding it.

Lying on the floor all around it are bodies. Unmoving bodies. Too many of them. Women and men alike, all with one arm tied up to the machine. As I get a closer look, each arm tied to the machine has a cut on it where the purple spell is pulling at it, taking their blood. Their magic.

This is what the Grand Chancellor meant by using people to make electricity? I want to retch. My heart aches in a way it never has before. It's heavy to the point it physically hurts, the pain overriding my senses.

One of the people on the floor's foot moves. I jump, grabbing onto Jack's arm. He gives my hand a pat and then walks over to the person who just moved. He whispers something I can't hear.

"All is well," he says louder. "We're here to help."

More people begin to stir. It's a good thing. They need to be able to move to get out of here, but seeing how alive these people are, what they are going through, is almost more than I can take.

Jack unhooks the machine attached to the foot mover's arm. The spell releases with the detachment. It spurs me into action. I fly to the machine and unhook as many of the people as quickly as I can. The others help, but it doesn't feel fast enough. We can't get away from this place soon enough.

Hoarse whispers of thanks are mingled with exhausted looks. The people are weak from their ordeal. Seeing them try and do something as simple as walking, seeing them struggle to put one foot in front of the other, to not fall to the ground, all of it makes my stomach sick.

I feel a torrent of rage at the Grand Chancellor for putting these people in this situation. It should never, ever have come about. He should have stuck to his trade routes with Chryos instead of ruining these people.

"How are we going to get them home?" I whisper to Jack.

He shakes his head. "One step at a time."

"And not get caught?" It's a formidable task. But one we have to succeed at.

We let them rest, giving them what food and water we have, though it's not nearly enough. They have been well fed, but with the strain of giving up so much magic and blood, it's not enough. Half an hour later, we decide that we can't wait any longer, no matter how much these people need rest. Here is not the place to let them have it.

Chadwick checks out front, then says, "It's clear."

Jack leads the way, herding the group of twenty-five people out of the building and through the expanse of nothing but dirt and weeds toward the forest. I help a woman in the middle who, despite the rest, can barely walk. Chadwick brings up the back, and the others are scattered throughout.

My heart is breaking as I try to help the woman while watching the others around me. What type of madman is the Grand Chancellor? Why would anyone help him do this?

We're about halfway to the forest when Jack calls out, "Run!"

He turns toward the right where a warlock is coming out of the forest opposite of where we're going. I pick up the woman I was helping and sprint to the forest. As soon as we're safely in the trees, I set her down. "Ask the first person who comes through here to give you a hand."

And I'm off, trying not to worry about her. There isn't time.

Cynthia, Lukas, and Chadwick are spelling the warlock who's now attacking them, while Jack is hurrying the people to the forest.

I rush toward the back of the group where two people have fallen behind. A burst of dark blue mixed with purple zips through the guarding spells and passes a few feet in front of me.

That was too close. I make it to the two stragglers. Both are thin, but with two of them I can't do any carrying. I put an arm under each of them, wincing at how scrawny they feel beneath my arms.

We take off running, the two are able to go faster now that I'm helping, but it's still not fast enough. A second spell slams into the woman on my left. She collapses to the ground, gasping. The other person I was helping yells for me to take care of the woman and does their best trotting toward the forest.

Drat my being too focused on the end goal. I dive toward the woman, doing my best to protect her from any more incoming spells. She coughs several times. No more spells come our way, but the others have a flurry flying around them. It looks as though a second warlock has joined our attacker.

"I'm fine," the woman gasps out.

She doesn't sound well at all, but I scoop her up in my arms and hustle toward the protection the forest offers. Jack is coming for the other person I was helping. We're the last four to make it to the forest.

Cynthia casts a spell so bright it's blinding. I can't see at all where I'm going, but I keep on running. As my vision comes back, I'm almost to the forest. I say a silent thanks that I didn't trip on the way over. As soon as I think that, I go flying toward the ground.

Time seems to slow. All I can think is curse my luck. I roll my body and the women I'm carrying so I'll land on my back with her on top. My back hits a sharp rock, and time speeds back up.

"Ow." Nothing wants to move. None of my body seems to understand the danger we're in, only pain. Sharp, jagged pain. The woman stands and tries to help me up. Her feeble attempts aren't nearly enough to get me off the ground, but they are enough to get my body to remember the urgency we're under.

"I'm fine. Get to the forest." She hesitates only a moment before following my direction.

Those we saved are all in the forest. Jack comes back, grabs my hand, and yanks me off the ground. "Don't you dare fall again."

As we run, I huff back, "I don't plan on it."

He puts a hand on my back, helping me toward the trees. As

soon as we make it, I turn toward the fight. Only, there is no more fight. The warlocks are both on the ground and the others are running toward us. But not all are well. Chadwick is cradling his left arm like it's been injured.

"Keep them going," Cynthia yells.

Jack races into action. It takes me a moment longer. My instinct says to check on Chadwick, to see how injured he is. But he's a grown man. He can take care of himself for the moment while I help others who need my help more than he does. I turn and follow Jack, helping him to get the people moving.

Behind us, Cynthia calls out. I turn toward her. She's running toward us, two forms on the ground behind her.

"Go!" she yells.

The lumps on the ground don't get up to follow. Jack slows to cover our tracks, and Cynthia helps him. I stay where I am, helping the people move on. It's going to be a very long journey back to the cave, especially if we're avoiding capture.

CHAPTER 39

I t takes several days to return to the cave, but we eventually make it in the end. Whether it's due to not being chased or Cynthia and Jack's excellent track-covering skills, we aren't followed. Chadwick's arm is tender, but not as badly injured as I first suspected and easily fixed. All in all, it was a fairly successful, if not what I was expecting, break out.

The hardest trick is not thinking on what I saw. My dreams are nothing but nightmares now. Me locked up to that horrid machine. Or worse yet, those I care about locked up to the machine and being unable to help them.

The nightmares continue to haunt me as Bethany, Cynthia, Tawny, and Serena help me get the newest members settled. Good places to rest and plenty of food and drink. More than we can afford to give them, really, but with their weakened state, I don't know how we can't give it to them.

As I hand one man a bowl of stew, tears fill his eyes. "Thank you for saving us."

"It was the least we could do," I reply, my own eyes tearing in response. "You shouldn't have been put in that situation anyway."

"No, I shouldn't have. No one should be," he says. "Do you know why I was put in there?"

"I don't."

"Because I owed the Grand Chancellor a partly sum of money."

"That's it?" I ask, not knowing what else to say when this burning rage fills me. "He's clearly a madman."

"The worst there ever was."

His words continue to haunt me as I dish out more food to men and women. What were they all taken for? Not paying their bills? No matter what you can or can't pay, your life force shouldn't be the consequence.

I scrape the last bit of stew from the pot, and my belly growls. At least there was enough for those we just found. They need it more than I do, but at this rate, there won't be enough for even them. Food has always been a concern, but never this bad.

After handing out the last bowl, I gather the others helping me and have them follow me out of the cave. Once we're away from everyone else, I say, "We have to get more food. We're not going to survive without it."

"I didn't expect it to be this bad," Bethany says.

I'm just grateful she didn't see them in the power plant. "Neither did I."

"Where else can we get food, though?" Serena asks. "We're already getting as much as we can and it's getting more risky every time we try."

"We could try hitting a farm instead of the markets," Cynthia says.

"But would that get the farmers in trouble?" Bethany asks.

"No more than it's gotten the shop owners in trouble," Serena says.

A cloud of darkness descends. Helping a nation find its way is not going very smoothly. "We're going to have to do something. As much as I don't want anyone else to get in trouble because of us, we have to feed these people, or we'll never survive and the Grand Chancellor will win."

Cynthia says, "A farm it is."

* * *

AFTER A COUPLE WEEKS OF SEARCHING, we've found the perfect farm to hit. Lots of food nearby, vegetables and much needed fruit and only a farmer and one helper running it. We gather as many as we can to help us. We're not leaving anything to chance. The more help we have, the less likely we will be to lose, and land's knows we can't afford to lose.

The attack is not really an attack. We go in there, spells blazing —or ready to. Our hands are all up to cast a spell when we come across the first farmer.

"Whoa," he says. "Don't go blasting me yet."

I don't lower my arm. "Why not?"

"You're that group I've been hearing about, yes? The one trying to fight the Grand Chancellor?"

"So what if we are?"

"If so, I want to help you all out."

Finally, I lower my hand. "Help us out how and why?"

"You need food, right? Otherwise, you wouldn't be here."

"Yes, but that doesn't answer the why." I take a few steps toward him, even if everyone else is still on guard behind me.

"Been sick of the Grand Chancellor's rule for a long time. Had to send my oldest boy into service at his house to pay off a debt. Don't fancy my children being taken from me like that, even if they are nearly grown. Especially not with all I do to try and provide food for the country. I reckon if I'm going to give food to someone, it might as well be someone who can help."

I motion the others to lower their hands. This man is anything but a threat. "We are definitely trying to help."

"Then how about this. I can give you half of my food stored up now, and I'll do what I can to help you out in the future."

"That's more than generous," I say.

It takes a little arranging, but we figure out how to pack up all the food he offers and carry it out of there. Before we go, I tell him, "Thank you for your help. This will help more than you know."

"Does that mean you have a lot of mouths to feed?"

"It does."

"Good then. I hope the Grand Chancellor gets what's coming to him."

"And what will you do if the Grand Chancellor finds out you've been helping us?"

"You let me worry about that."

I put my hand out to shake his. "Please stay safe."

He shakes my hand. "You too."

After making arrangements to collect more food in the future, we leave. I think we're doing exactly what we need to. More people come too. Even those we think we're going to fight with, instead want to help us like the farmer. The Grand Chancellor has overstepped, and even Chardonian warlocks know it.

CHAPTER 40

A thrill hums through me, both anxious and excited, as we ready to attack the next power plant. I'm excited that we are going to be able to help more people, although anxious to see what's to come. The first time was difficult. At least this time I'm more prepared. We all are, plus we brought more help this time.

Though this place is much closer and has more forest around it for us to hide in, it has the same spells fortifying it as the last one. It's probably the setup for all of them, though you think they'd add at least a few more spells after our last attack. Maybe they added guards instead.

The building looks the same with its red brick, no windows, and wires coming out the top, but it's set in a forest this time. A lot more places to hide before running across open terrain.

"Let's see what they've got waiting for us," Cynthia says.

She leads us through the spells, taking us through faster than last time. When we get to the building, it's the same drill as before. All of us line up against the wall, pulling out the red side of our material Katherine made so we blend in more.

Jack waits until we're all in place, then knocks on the door. No answer. He knocks again. Still no one answers. He knocks a third time.

He looks to me, and I shrug. Does this mean they're waiting for us inside? Ready to jump on us the moment we enter? Or are there no guards?

I scoot across the wall so I'm closer to him but still won't be easily seen since the door opens next to me, and I'm leaning against the wall. I lift my hand, just in case he needs immediate reinforcement. But when he opens the door, nothing happens.

He points at Chadwick and himself, and then inside. Chadwick moves forward, but I shake my head. There's no way they're both going in there alone. I hold my hands out, wrists together like they're cuffed, and then point at myself going in. Chadwick has the gall to huff, but Cynthia jumps right in, spelling both of our wrists to look like they are tied together with a spell, but in reality, it's just a burst of light.

Jack leads us in, Chadwick bringing us in from behind. He may be the strongest warlock present, but there's no telling how he'd be mistaken for a Chardonian. He's over a head taller than I am, and compared to the Chardonians, I'm pretty tall. Still, it's nice to know his skills are with us.

It's even nicer to know that Jack is leading us. There's something so safe and secure about him. The people he cares about, he cares for deeply. What's more, he's quick on his feet. I know with him guiding us, we're in the best possible hands.

We enter the glaringly bright hall. It's empty. Why aren't there any guards here? Are there no people here to rescue? I can't think why else, and my suspicion only increases as we turn the corner and find the same sickening setup as last time. Even though I saw the sight before, a gasp escapes me.

Several of those locked up look our way. One says, "Don't come in." But it's too late. As soon as Jack's foot crosses the line into the room, a multitude of spells spring into life. It's a trap.

Reds, blues, blacks, purples all surround us in a dizzying array.
"No one move," Cynthia says.

Not like I was planning on it. Even an inch in any direction, and I'll hit a spell. Some spells separate us from each other, even.

"Do you know if anyone's here?" Jack calls out toward the woman who first spoke.

"Not now. They'll be coming now that you've sprung their spells, though."

Chadwick curses.

Cynthia doesn't wait. She's already breaking through the spells between us while Chadwick is working on the ones behind us.

I help Cynthia smash the spells between us and then work towards the people.

"Just leave us," a woman calls out. "Don't get captured because of us."

"Speak for yourself," a man replies. "I want out of here so I can pay the Grand Chancellor back for his treachery."

That statement alone makes me work faster trying to get to them. That is exactly the sort of person we need on our side.

Behind us, Chadwick yells, "We have to go. Now!"

"We can't," I yell back, trying not to think about how exhausted I am and how low my magic is running.

"There's too many warlocks coming, and they'll be here before you can break through."

"But we can't leave them."

"Just go," one of them calls out.

"I can't." I hack away at another spell, a frenzied urgency gripping me.

Jack puts his arms around me, dragging me backward. "We can't save anyone if we get caught ourselves."

He's right. Oh, so right. But leaving them here like this... "I'll be back for you as soon as I can."

"Save yourself now, then," the man calls out. "And hurry back."

The statement has me turning toward the exit, but not without a pricking in my chest. Jack hurries me toward the exit that Chadwick has already cleared and Cynthia waits at with the others, huddled just inside the door. Everyone is staring out the door. When I peek to see why, my breath leaves in a painful gasp.

Outside, a small army of warlocks waits for us.

CHAPTER 41

"What do we do now?" I ask.

Theodore gives me a look.

"What? It's not like ignoring them will make them go away."

"What about the spell you used to escape Stephen before?" Lukas asks Cynthia. "If we could all fly away on a spell, that would work."

"I'm not strong enough to carry this many people. I barely did it when it was just you and me," she replies.

"What if we all work together?"

She shakes her head. "I don't think we'll have enough power to get far enough away fast enough."

"Any other ideas?" Jack asks.

"We need something as a distraction," I say. "Something big. I think I know just the thing. Firework spells. Only aimed at them instead of at the sky."

"It could work," Cynthia says. "We'll have to throw as many as we can, and get out of here as fast as we can, covering our tracks as we go."

"I can cover our tracks," Jack says. "It's the one thing I'm good at."

"Good. You take the rear. The rest of you, on the count of three, send as many firework spells at the army as you can. Put some on delay if possible." Cynthia crouches as if readying to run, and I do the same. "One. Two. Three."

I push out the spell as hard and fast as I can, exploding colors in front of them so hopefully they can't see us. And run. I stay toward the back of the group by Jack, ready to defend him if need be. While we run, I throw out more firework spells. The bigger the better, as many as I possibly can. I've never put so much into what I once thought was a frivolous spell before. We run and run, making it to the cover of the trees.

The flashing lights can be seen in glimpses as we go but fade with each footstep. I stay close to Jack as he slows to cover our tracks with a muddy brown spell. It fills them in with dirt from the surrounding areas.

A maroon spell whizzes just over our heads, slamming into a tree behind us, making it explode.

"Faster," I say.

"I can only go so fast."

"Let me help." I cover our tracks just ahead of him with a tan spell that leaves things almost all hidden, but not perfectly. He comes after and wipes the rest away, hiding everything from view.

"Good. Now you move faster," he says.

I grunt and hurry as quickly as I can, but my power is tired after all those firework spells, and I've always struggled with track-covering spells. My power aches within me, struggling to do the spell. At least it seems to be helping Jack to go faster, which was the point.

The lights are getting further away now. The noise of the army is dimming. We're going to make it out of this trap. We'll make it back home, and hopefully be back here to save these people another day. A day in the near future, I hope.

Suddenly, a bronze spell smacks into Jack's leg. He lets out a hiss.

"What can I do?" I ask, wondering how bad it is.

"Keep going," he replies through gritted teeth.

I continue on, but look for the target who hit Jack. Nothing is in sight but trees now, and the group ahead of us we're working to hide the tracks of. Only a few seconds later, another bronze spells spits out, this time coming straight for me. I dive away from it, but not in time. It sizzles against my hand, leaving it burning.

"You all right?" Jack asks, voice still strained.

"As much as you are," I reply, pain lacing my words.

Cynthia is suddenly at our side, helping us with hiding everyone's tracks. If we could just move fast enough to lose this last hex we'll make it. Between the three of us, the work goes a lot faster. Until I spot another bronze spell coming our way.

"Down," I call out, but not loud enough to carry.

All three of us dodge to the ground. I pop back up as soon as the spell flies overhead and aim a sleep spell at where the bronze spell came from. The power blue light flashes through the air, hitting the culprit, knocking him to the ground.

"Nice shot," Cynthia says as she continues covering our tracks.

No one else follows, though the run out is scary. The three of us start the track-hiding spell back up. By the time we have been running for what seems like hours, it finally appears safe enough to stop.

"What happened inside?" Annabelle asks.

"That was a bad trap," I respond. "We're going to need an entirely different approach. I don't know if we can hit another power plant for a while."

My heart aches to think of all those we left behind. Those that were in such horrendous circumstances.

"How can we not go back?" Cynthia asks.

"Because we'll just end up right beside them," I say. "We'll be no use to them there."

"None of it's acceptable," Chadwick says.

"Agreed," Jack replies. "But we won't do anything but get

caught if we stand around here talking instead of getting home safe. Let's move."

And we all listen, getting a move on toward what's become home. But I have a feeling the nightmares I had about the power plants before will be nothing in comparison to what I'll have now. As well I should.

CHAPTER 42

I collapse onto my bed, completely worn and unwilling to move again for months. Fine, I'll have to move before then. One does need to use the necessity and eat, but that doesn't mean I have to move any more than that.

More than physically exhausted, I'm emotionally drained. How could we just leave all those people behind? I know it would have been our capture had we not, but it's the worst kind of struggle to get the image of them out of the forefront of my mind. How can one human treat another human so cruel?

"Knock, knock," a male voice sounds just outside my shared room.

Inwardly, I groan. The last thing I want right now is someone else around. "Come in."

Jack rounds the corner and leans against the archway leading into my room but doesn't say anything. My heartbeat quickens. "Is there something I can help you with?"

"I was just wondering if…"

I sit up. "Yes?"

"If you would like to talk. About what just happened."

The ache deep within me grows heavier, like a rock pile that just keeps having more and more rocks added to it. It's something I want to ignore and never think on again. But something about his manner, his presence leaves me wanting to speak despite myself. "Why don't you come in? Have a seat. Cynthia won't mind if you borrow her bed. I'm sorry we don't have any chairs."

"We don't have much of anything in here." He moves to the very end of Cynthia's bed, the end closest to me, and sits on the edge. I expect him to say something more, but he doesn't. He just waits.

"I don't know if I'll ever forgive myself for leaving them behind," is what finally comes out of my mouth.

Even though he's already on the edge of the bed, he scoots closer. "We didn't have a choice."

"I know that. I do. But they don't have a choice either. They're chained to a machine that sucks their magic from them even as they make it. It's horrifying, and we left them there. I just left them there."

"Because I dragged you away."

"You had to. Otherwise I wouldn't have left."

"Which means if anyone is at fault, it's me."

I scoot to the end of my bed, closer to him. "You saved my life."

"So you can try to save theirs again someday. Hopefully soon."

"You're right." But still I feel deflated. "We just don't have enough people or magic behind us to defeat the Grand Chancellor and his men."

"Don't you dare give up now."

I flop back down on my bed. "But how can we not? This was a hopeless task before it even started."

"You don't really mean that."

"But I do. If I and the other Sanos hadn't interfered with Chardonia, things wouldn't be this bad."

"Yet, where would I be?"

I sigh and shake my head.

"No, I mean it," he persists. "Where would I be? What type of person would I be like?"

I can't help it. I sit up and give him a wry grin. "You'd be ornerier than an old man."

He laughs. "Not just that, but I'd not respect women like they deserve."

"Plus, Serena would have never met Zade and would be under the control of some horrid warlock, and Cynthia would never have shown so many Chardonians she could do magic in the first place. She may have even been caught doing magic and been sacrificed and had all memories of her erased by those she cared about."

"Exactly," he says. The tone of his voice becomes more serious and deeper. "And I wouldn't have met you."

My heart flutters. My stomach becomes light, giddy. Is this what falling in love feels like?

We lean closer to each other. And closer. Are we going to kiss? I want to kiss him. I want to know what it feels like to have a man's lips pressed against mine. To feel my heart soar higher than the clouds.

Is this what falling in love feels like? Sunshine in my chest, lighting to a fire at the thought of a kiss and roaring into a heated passion as our lips meet? This is more than I ever hoped I would feel. I pull Jack closer, not wanting the moment to end.

There are footsteps before I even have time to register them. Someone is coming. Cynthia appears. Drat this place and it not having any privacy.

"I'm, uh, interrupting I think," Cynthia says. "I'll just go."

She's gone before I have a chance to tell her to stay. It's just as well. I probably wouldn't have said it anyway, despite all the politeness my mother drilled into me because the last thing I want right now is someone else around. Even if the mood is already gone. We've both pulled back. No finding out what it's like to kiss him. At least not right now.

It's just as well. Kissing a man is serious business. If I'm going to kiss him, I want to make sure it's what we both really want. Though it's hard to think that right here and now with us both leaning back in toward each other. With the way he's gazing at my lips like they are the most important object in all the world.

Forget thinking about things. I want that kiss.

I stand, and he does so as well, only I move the few paces to him, put a hand on each side of his face, and kiss him. It happens so fast, I almost don't believe I actually did it. But his lips are pressed to mine and mine to his. His arms wrap around me, pulling me in closer.

I never knew a kiss could feel like this. Warm and good, with the flutters from earlier racing up and down my entire body. I never want it to end. And it doesn't. It just goes on with burning heat.

Someone clears their throat. We yank apart with sudden coldness. It grows even colder when I see who interrupted us. Chadwick.

"Um...hi." Most awkward moment. Ever. "How can I help you?"

He glances at Jack, no, more like a glare, and then looks back at me. "I just wanted to make sure you're well after everything that happened. But I can see I shouldn't have come. I'll talk to you later."

He turns to leave. I call after him, "Chadwick, wait."

But he's already gone.

"I should be going as well," Jack says.

Oh lovely, now he's upset too. I'd rather kiss more than deal with two ornery men. But Jack's already gone as well. Everything feels all twisted up. Wrong. Why can't things be simple? Love is hard. Anything is easier than romance. All I know anymore is that Jack's right. Helping the Chardonian people is the best thing I could be doing.

CHAPTER 43

The natural spring running through what we've turned into the kitchen has icy cold water. Katherine scrubs pots next to me. She returned just this morning and is already helping with chores. She doesn't even have to be doing any since she's only visiting and doesn't live here, yet she's jumped in to help anyway. If only it was as easy to get the people who are supposed to help to do so. Not that they don't. Most of them are pretty good, but a few stubborn ones don't seem to understand what we provide for them.

"Only three more to go," Katherine says, heaving the large pot to me to dry off.

"So, tell me a little bit about this Charles you brought with you."

Her cheeks instantly redden.

There's a blush if I ever saw one. "I knew it. How did you two meet?"

She sombers, the red leaving her cheeks and making them look whiter under the torchlight. "I ran away from home and met him on the streets. He saved me from a fate worse than death."

"Dare I ask what that fate might have been?"

"Marrying a wretched old man who smelled rancid." She shivers.

I put a hand on her shoulder. "I'm glad you found him."

She gives me a soft grin then hands me another pot. We quickly finish up the last of the dishes and put them away. We walk toward the main cavern.

A girl of about nineteen, just older than me, says, "Hello, Waverly."

"Are you doing well today?"

"Grand. Cynthia just showed me a hex that knocks warlocks asleep."

"That one is useful. Can I introduce you to my friend, Katherine?" I nod in her direction.

The girl's face goes blank. "I'm sorry. I don't see anyone here but you."

They start to walk away, but I stop her. "You can't just walk away from someone like that."

"There's no one here but you, and I thought we were done with our conversation."

"But I just introduced you to Katherine."

Her gaze scans over her very briefly, so quick I almost missed it. "She's less than a shadow, not worth noticing."

She storms off. I move to go after her, but Katherine grabs my arm. "Don't. It's not worth it."

"It is. They shouldn't treat you like that. Not after all you're doing to pitch in and help."

"No, they shouldn't. But there's a lot of things that shouldn't be. Besides, being less than a shadow has its advantages."

Still, she shouldn't be treated that way. But I guess after dealing with so many bad things, it's hard to believe in the good. At least I assume that's what's holding them back because there's no other reason for them to ignore Katherine so thoroughly, especially when she's only trying to help.

"They'll come around," I say. "It took a while with me. They probably just need more time with you as well."

"I wish they would. There's so much more help I could offer if I knew they would trust it."

I give her a quick squeeze. "I know. Why don't I introduce you to our leader? He was gone last time you visited. He should be happier to see you."

I take her to find him, asking around where he is to discover he's outside. We find him, back to us, sitting on a fallen tree trunk.

"Jack," I say. "I have someone I'd like you to meet."

He stands and turns, but before I can say anything, he drops the piece of wood he was whittling and stares at Katherine. She stares back, face pale between her inked lines.

"Do you know Katherine?"

Still, neither say anything.

After another moment, Jack finally says, "This is my sister. The one I told you about."

"Katherine?"

"It's true," she replies and then says to him, "What are you doing here?"

"Trying to help. Trying to make amends for the way I treated you growing up. Can you ever forgive me?"

Her brows knit together like she's lost. "I didn't expect to ever see you again. And if I did, I didn't expect you to recognize me like this." She motions to her face and bald head.

"Your image is engrained into my memory. I could never forget someone I so cruelly mistreated."

"When did you decide that it was cruel? You used to think it was normal."

"After I came to work for Councilman Daniel. I began to see that even though he was a councilman, he treated everyone with respect, including his wife. It made me wonder if I was taught wrong all those years. If I mistreated you for no purpose. Then I met Waverly. She quickly convinced me that women are of much greater worth than I ever knew."

The silence that follows is only broken by the chirping of a bird.

"It's not an easy thing to forgive," Katherine finally says.

"I understand. I will work to earn your forgiveness the best I can."

She steps closer to him. "You already have it."

I can't help but smile as I watch the two reunite.

CHAPTER 44

Jack should be rounding everyone up for a meeting any minute now. Jack, Katherine's brother. I wouldn't have guessed it, though I don't think either of them would have either. At least some hopeful things are coming out of all this mess.

I flash a mirror spell out, a reflective silver that smooths out before me, shinier than a real mirror but just as effective. I run a second spell, which turns out a bright red, to brush through my hair. The long locks are stubborn but probably only because I so badly want them to behave.

Once my hair's done, I bite my lips, reddening them, and then add the faintest bit of a spell to my eyelids. A faint white one that shimmers in the light. Not that there's much light here in the cave. There's the echo of footsteps approaching.

I zip my mirror away and stand. Nerves flutter through me like firework spells. I've never been so affected by a warlock before. Who knew it would be a Chardonian warlock that would be the one to do it?

The echoes are closer now. I take a deep breath, hold it, and slightly part my lips. The steps turn the corner.

"Expecting someone else?" Cynthia says.

I let out the breath in a huff and zip the glitter off my eyelids. That was going a bit far anyway, especially for someone like Jack. "Of course not."

She laughs. "I'm sure you weren't. Jack sent me to get you."

"Oh."

"Don't sound so deflated. He got trapped into a conversation with Theodore. I'm certain he would much rather have come for you himself."

Heat tickles my cheeks. "It's just a meeting."

"Where you two will pretend it's all about business, while the rest of us wonder when you'll finally just kiss. I swear, the tension between you two almost needs to be dealt with as much as this war."

I can't help but giggle, not mentioning we have kissed. Oh lands, have we kissed. "My, you've sure grown up since meeting Lukas."

"And you're about to grow up just as much."

I laugh harder before sobering. "It's hard to think about a relationship with everything else going on."

"Trust me, I know. But I think we all need extra love while the world is so bleak."

The thought turns me silent. Maybe, just maybe, she could be right.

"We should go. A certain someone will turn grumpy if we don't show up soon, and we both know when he turns grumpy, you turn grumpy."

I chuckle. "You have a point."

We head out of the room and into the large cavern to meet with all the people. Its large space isn't covered even a quarter of the way with people. The people here are eager and willing to help, but it's just not enough.

We hurry from the room to a smaller cavern where we leaders

meet. Jack is there. I can't help but blush remembering everything Cynthia said about him.

"We need more people. This group isn't enough. Not if we're going to save people from the power plants." Frustration bubbles in me. "There has to be something we can do."

Cynthia stands. "There is. I will go around the country and find more people loyal to our cause."

"You can't," Serena says, jumping to her feet as well. "It's too dangerous."

"What do you think I've been doing for the last several months?"

Serena looks to me. I shrug. "I agree that it is dangerous, but we're running out of options. We either give up now or give it everything we have now because that's what it's going to take."

The silence that encompasses us is heavy, wrought with the unknown of what's to come. We're barely surviving this rebellion. I don't want anything bad to come of anyone, but without more help, it will be a lost cause.

"You're correct," Serena says. "And I'm coming with you."

"You needn't risk you're life too," Cynthia counters.

"We've seen how the people react to both of us. It will be more effective if I come with you than if you go alone."

"I can't argue with that," Cynthia says. "And it will be good to have a sister with me."

"It's settled then," I say, trying not to think on how Zade would react to this all. Maybe he'd surprise me and be in support. If anything, he'd insist on going with them, but I can't afford that luxury, not to mention all the people I'd scare off. "But you two had both better stay safe. Don't you dare take any more risks than you absolutely have to."

Cynthia shrugs. Of course she won't be able to guarantee that.

"We won't," Serena says, solidifying the fact that Cynthia needs her as much as she needs to go with Cynthia.

"I think we need more than just who you two can gather," I say.

"I think we need someone to go gather those we've sent back into society. Someone they'll trust to know it's time to come back and fight."

"I'll go," Chadwick says.

"Or I can," Theodore says. "I should not only be a familiar face, but a familiar countryman."

As much as I want to send Chadwick, Theodore has a point. Besides, I can't decide why, exactly, it is that I want to send Chadwick, and I need to be sure it's for the good of the people. "Theodore, I think you'd be the best fit for the job."

"Thank you. I will send back as many warlocks as I can to help."

"We should pack our things and move out before the day is over," Cynthia says.

I grab Serena and Cynthia with one arm and pull them into a group hug. "I will miss you both so much."

"And we'll miss you," Serena says.

CHAPTER 45

I t's quiet without Cynthia to share a room with. Or what
passes for our room in any case. It's quieter still when I help at
practice. Without Cynthia and Serena, nothing is the same.

The week moves slowly. Training others. Helping with chores
around the place. An uneventful trip for food. Everything falls
into place, as long as it's contained within our own little world.

I stare at the target my group of trainees are trying to hit, and
it blurs into mush. There's no excitement around. No fun.
Nothing but everyone taking a deep breath in the hopes that soon
we will win this war.

I shake myself out of it. I can't ignore those who need my help
as much as I'm tired and ready for a break. As much as I wish my
friends were back, with all the help we desperately need.

I walk down the line of girls and one warlock. He didn't have
anywhere to go, so he stayed here when most others were sent
back into society. He doesn't need much encouragement. He hits
his target every time with a different type of spell.

The next girl is doing all right. I give her a few pointers, which
she quickly takes. The next in line is Phyllis. She's standing,
staring at the target like I was doing only moments before. Hope-

fully, her thoughts are more pleasant than mine, but judging by the frown on her face, it's unlikely.

"How are you doing?" I ask her.

She glances up at me before looking back at her target. "I'm fine."

I move a little closer and lower my voice. "Are you sure? Is there anything you'd like to talk about? Anything I can help you with?"

She mumbles something I can't make out.

"What was that?"

She shakes her head. "I don't know that I like practicing magic. It feels...wrong."

"Wrong how? Maybe we just need to adjust the way you're doing something."

"I don't think that's it."

"What do you think it is, then?"

She lets out a long breath. "I know what you all say, and I know what I've seen all of you do, but magic is meant for warlocks. Men. Not someone like me."

"You're worth more than you think. You can do this. I know you can."

She says nothing, her mouth making a thin line.

"Why don't you show me a spell? Nothing fancy, just a burst of pure magic?" Not only will it help me gauge how she's doing with her spell casting, but the color of light might give me a better indication of her mood.

She holds up her hand like she's getting ready to cast a spell, only nothing happens. A moment later, she drops her hand. "I'm sorry. I just can't do it."

I put a hand on her shoulder. "That's all right. We can try again later." Though I think we'd better not take her on any fights. Not if she can't bring herself to do even a simple spell here.

"Do you really think we can do it?" she asks.

"Do what?"

"Win the war against the Grand Chancellor?"

Though I'm questioning it myself, I don't dare say anything of the sort to her. "Of course we can."

"What will happen to us if we can't? Will we be tarnished?"

I look at her, really look. I can't sugar coat it any more than I already have. She's been punished before, and she knows what this country is like better than I do. Why else would she have spied on Serena instead of befriending her? I know she would have been tarnished if she hadn't told on Serena to Stephen. She's faced it before and came out better than she went in. She can do it again.

"I'm afraid being tarnished would be the least of our worries if we lose," I say. "But honestly, I don't know exactly what will happen to us."

She nods, more solemn than when I first started talking to her. "If you don't mind, I think I'm done practicing for the day."

"Of course," I reply. "Please let me know if there's anything you want to talk about."

She nods, but the way she presses her lips together makes me wonder if she really will.

After she leaves, I continue helping the others for another hour. Finally, I release them all, and Tawny goes with them to hopefully do something relaxing. I can't bring myself to move. After talking to Phyllis, I'm feeling extra downtrodden.

Chadwick walks over, bringing me a drink. "Care to talk about it?"

"Talk about what?"

"Whatever it is that's bothering you. What's making you act so un-Waverly like."

"What good will talking about it do? Those people will still be trapped in power plants across the country. The Grand Chancellor will still be in power. Cynthia and Serena will still be gone. I just don't see how talking helps."

"Coming from the girl who used to love to do nothing but

talk." When I don't respond, he sighs. "I just want you to be happy, and I don't know how to help you get there."

"I don't know how to get there either. It's like some unobtainable thing."

"Do you ever miss the days before we joined Sanos? Back when we were in Chardonia, just me you, Zade and Tawny?"

It's a hard question to answer. "Of course I miss it. The peace and freedom. But not so much I wish to go back. I wouldn't change helping these people or knowing Serena and her family." Or Jack. Why did that thought just pop into my head? Guilt pings inside me knowing I thought that when Chadwick was sitting right here. But why should it? It's not as if Chadwick and I have an agreement. And there definitely isn't anything going on between me and Jack. Or is there?

"You look very concerned," Chadwick says. "What are you thinking about?"

"Just the weather."

"In other words, you're not going to tell me."

"Nope."

He chuckles. "Some things never change."

"But most things do."

That sobers him. "Tell me. Did you not send me to gather the warlocks because I'm Envadi or because of something else? Something that's not going on between us?"

The question stabs at my emotions. "It would have been hard because you're an Envadi."

He steps closer. "But?"

I step back. "I'm sorry, Chadwick. That's all."

"Oh. I see," he says. "It's because of Jack, isn't it?"

Heat immediately creeps up my face. "No. At least not entirely."

"And what is that supposed to mean?"

"It means that while yes, I care for Jack—" Just thinking about him sends my heart pounding harder. "It wouldn't have worked between us anyway."

"Waverly, I was wo—" Tawny comes to a halt several feet from us. "I'm sorry. Am I interrupting?"

Chadwick looks at me, his face tight with pain. "No. Apparently there's nothing to interrupt."

He leaves, steps heavy as he goes. Once his footsteps have faded, Tawny says, "I did bother you two, didn't I?"

I shrug and wish there was a way to disappear at this moment. "I'm grateful you came when you did."

"And why is that?"

"It was getting very uncomfortable. And now he knows how I feel."

"Don't feel too bad, Waverly. Even back in Envadi, when everyone was pushing you two to get together, it felt like the pull between you two was coming only from his side."

"Really? I always felt so confused about it."

"And being confused is exactly what the problem is." She gets a sly grin. "You don't seem confused about Jack."

For the second time today, my face heats. "No, I'm not confused by him. More like confused by the situation we've been put in."

She sighs. "It's not easy. Hopefully with all the help Serena, Cynthia, and Theodore are rounding up, it won't be much longer before we're out of this situation."

"And what if it is? What if this whole plan falls apart?"

"We'll deal with that if it comes."

I give her a hug. "Thank you for all of this. I don't know what I would have done if you didn't come with me."

"You would have done a lot more training by yourself and not known nearly as many spells."

"That's all too true," I say. "It's what I get for slacking off in class."

"You weren't the only one. I just had tutors that wouldn't leave me alone until I got something down."

"Spoiled."

"Hey, now. That's a low blow."

"But a true one."

She laughs, and I join in, feeling good to get everything out.

"Do you think they'll be able to find enough people to help?" she asks.

"They'll have to."

Because if they don't, our lives will be forfeited.

CHAPTER 46

S erena, Cynthia, and Theodore's return isn't just a joyous thing, it's a celebration. The people they've been sending home, plus the people they brought with them, will go a long, long ways to helping defeat the Grand Chancellor. There are more people than I expected. Our caves are so filled with people. It's getting hard to find places to put them all.

Best yet is just knowing this many people want the Grand Chancellor out of power. When I first came to Chardonia, I never thought it would be possible. These people are a surprising joy.

We don't waste any time meeting together with the core leaders. Jack is sitting next to me as I look everyone over. Something about his presence sticks out in my mind more than I expect. But we need to get this meeting underway.

I ask, "Where should we hit first? The power plant again? Or Chancellor Stephen's house?"

Serena and Cynthia glance at each other, a spark in their eyes. But Bethany is the one who surprises me. "Chancellor Stephen's. He needs to be taken down several notches. Plus, it will be a more visible attack to the people of Chardonia than a power plant, which only affects the upper class."

Inside, I'm cheering for her strength, even though I'm anxious to save those people.

"Isn't Chancellor Stephen your father?" Tawny asks.

"He is," Bethany says. "But the only thing he ever gave us of any use was with my mother's help, and that is for us to be alive. Everything else he's done, no parent should ever do to a child."

I can't help it. I put my arm around Bethany. "Attacking his house is a definite yes."

* * *

STEPHEN'S HOUSE looms over us. It's dark and unprotected, at least as far as spells I can see go.

"Nathaniel did say that he wouldn't be home tonight, right?" I ask.

"Yes," Bethany replies.

"But what if he's just sleeping?" Serena asks.

"Then we'll face him head on," Cynthia says.

"And we'll do it if we have to," Bethany says.

Yet, they all just stand there.

"Who wants to go first?" I ask.

No one responds.

"Maybe I can start, then, by getting all the servants out of the house."

"That'd be a good idea," Serena says.

"Yeah, I can't help with that," Cynthia adds.

Soon, all three of them are rounding up servants. I'm surprised at how the servants react. Instead of fleeing, the servants are happy to see them. Not just happy, thrilled.

"We've missed you so much," one of the servants says. "We've been so worried about you."

When the house is all clear of people, there's more standing around just staring at the house, only this time with the servants.

"Should I start?" I ask, wondering what it will take to get them going.

"No, no," Cynthia says. "We should do it."

Still, they stare. The first person to finally move surprises me. Bethany. She holds up her hand and, with a burst of red light, crashes through a window pane. Serena follows by breaking down the door, and then Cynthia knocks out the rest of the windows. Soon, all three of them are working on the house until it's up in flames. Even after it's on fire, they shoot more and more blasting spells at it. They delight in burning down the house.

After this success, we take down two more power plants. We rescue several dozens of people, and stop the production of electricity by not just taking the power source but destroying the building. We lose a few members who become prisoners according to Nathaniel, but not nearly as many as we gain.

The Grand Chancellor may be powerful and have allies, but we have purpose. We are strong and more numerous than he expects. We will take back what belongs to the people.

CHAPTER 47

K atherine's face is pulled down in a somber expression. Too somber for a girl who's supposed to be in love and just found a brother who she's making amends with. I sit on the log next to her, gazing out into the forest.

"I'm sorry the people still aren't treating you better," I say.

She sighs, heavier than the clouds above us. "Posh. I mean I wish they would, but that's not the problem."

"Is it Jack?"

A smile tickles her lips. "No. I'm glad to have found him and glad he found you. He's become a much better person than the one I knew growing up."

"Then what is it?"

"Charles."

"Are you two having problems? You always look so in love when you're together."

"We are. That's the problem." She sighs again, even heavier than the last. "I so badly want to marry him. I'm tired of things getting in the way."

"Well, why don't you? A wedding may be just what we need."

"Everyone is so consumed with this war. It doesn't seem right to have a wedding."

"Maybe that's exactly why we do need one."

That silences her. The somber lines of her face recede, her face taking on a glow. We sit a minute in silence when Charles walks out.

"I think I'll leave you two alone," I say.

As I leave, I can't help but sneak a glance back. Katherine's face is glowing up at Charles. I think everything is going to be all right.

* * *

"I THINK we need to go back and rescue those people from the power plant," I say.

"Do you think it's safe after last time?" Tawny asks.

"Maybe not, but those people need to be saved." I can't get their faces out of my mind.

"It was hard to leave them behind," Jack says.

"Exactly. We have to go after them."

"What if you're caught?" Bethany says. "It feels like things are getting more and more dangerous with each attack you do. I'm not sure we can afford to keep attacking them."

"We haven't been caught yet," I say. "I think it's worth the risk."

"I tend to agree with Bethany," Serena says. "As much as I want to help those people, I fear we're pushing things too much. The Grand Chancellor is strong."

She shudders, and it's then that I remember just how much she's seen the Grand Chancellor up close. Not a lot, but more than the rest of us. I've only seen him in the distance at tournaments. I've never actually met the man. But she has. Not just that, but she's told stories of him sacrificing tarnished right in front of her.

Her grief when she told me becomes fresh in my mind. But then, so is the image of those suffering at the power plant, something she has yet to see for herself. "If you had seen the way those people suffer at the power plants, I think you would all agree with me that they need to be saved."

Serena's lips tighten while Bethany's eyes go wide. I'm grateful the babies are with Pernilla, even if they are too young to understand what we're talking about. Just having them about with this conversation would make me queasy. Or queasier rather. I'm already feeling sick at the thought of what the Grand Chancellor's done.

"Is it really that bad?" Serena asks, voice small.

"It's one of the worst things I've ever seen in my life," I say.

"The only thing worse," Cynthia adds, "was the sacrifice at the tournament."

Bethany says, "Maybe we should try. I'm just nervous for everyone's safety."

"It's something I've considered as well." More than I want to. There are too many people here that rely on us. "But I think it's worth the risk."

"It's worth a try," Theodore says.

"Agreed," Jack says. "We're stronger now, and those people need us."

"I think we should," Serena says. "As long as precautions are taken."

"Can we leave tomorrow?" I say.

"The sooner, the better," Cynthia says. "And this time, we'll all be prepared."

CHAPTER 48

Dusk is just brushing the sky when we look on the building. It looks so innocent from the outside. Nothing to hint at the atrocities going on in the inside. This time, there won't be any failure. I won't allow it.

"Let's move," I say.

Cynthia goes first. As much as I'd like to lead, it only makes sense to have the strongest of us take the front. Jack and I follow close behind with an even larger group behind us. There are about fifty of us, more than we've ever taken on a raid, but stealth is no longer an option. We will win this.

"There's someone on the side of the building," Theodore says from behind me.

"Cynthia?"

"I see him." A burst of purple light shoots from her to the right side of the building.

Then there's nothing.

"Did you get him?" I ask.

"I think so."

"We need to be sure."

"Stay here." She runs forward toward the side of the building,

Lukas darting after her. Despite her strength, he must not want her out of his sight. After our near capture the last time we were here, I don't blame him.

Only a short minute later, they both return. Cynthia says, "He's out."

I point toward the door, and we move out again. I wish we could just blast off the front of the building like we did the law office so long ago. With this many people, it'd be a breeze. But with the prisoners in there, we can't risk it.

As soon as we get to the door, we don't bother knocking. Lukas opens it, quickly moving out of the way while Cynthia stands at the ready, hands up. She blasts the warlock standing guard with another purple spell. He falls to the ground with a thunk.

Another warlock quickly takes his place. I beat Cynthia to hexing him to the ground. My skills have improved since our last encounter. He falls to the ground on top of the other warlock who is out cold, and my magic is still near full strength.

When no one else comes out, half of us pile in the building, the other half waiting outside to protect our backs. We meet five more warlocks in the hall, of which we take turns knocking out. I'm beginning to think we can do this when we make it to the main room.

The room is filled with not only the prisoners we meet before, but it's packed with warlocks, all of whom are surrounded by a bright yellow shield spell. I motion to those still in the hall to keep coming in. We're going to need all the firepower we can get.

"Give up now," one of the opposing warlocks says. "You can't win."

"On the contrary." I picture a sledgehammer coming down on their shield with more than enough force to break it and burst that image out in a gray spell speckled with green. It smashes against the shield, cracking it.

Others around me immediately follow suit, throwing spells at it to break it. Outwardly, I'm yelling praises and throwing more spells, but the shield is strong. And after we get through, if we get through, there are still the warlocks to contend with. What have we gotten ourselves into?

The opposing warlocks shoot spells at us, coming almost as fast as we're trying to take down their shield to reach them. My fingers go numb as I try to put a shield spell up in front of us. Too late. An orange spell zips through. I turn just in time to see it hit Theodore in the shoulder.

He collapses to the ground. I dive after him, readying to heal him if he is hurt bad enough. As I crouch beside him he says, "I'm fine."

Ignoring him, I brush aside his hand to see his charred shoulder beneath. The damage is severe, but something I can at least help with. I picture the skin's healing quickened, turning from a char to a pink to undamaged skin. The spell eases out in a soft red, straight for his shoulder. As it pours over his shoulder, I glance around to see if anyone else has fallen. No one. Even better, I find a way for the battle to lean in our favor.

Their shield doesn't go all the way to the ground.

"Are you well now?" I ask Theodore.

"Yes."

One less person to worry about. I want to grab Cynthia. She's the most powerful, but that also means she'd be the most notice-able loss. Instead I motion to Bethany, Jack, and a warlock whose name I don't know but has small ears. They crouch down beside me.

"There's a weak spot," I say, pointing to the feet of our oppo-nents, hope rising in me for the first time since we entered this room. "Attack there."

As one, we turn and shoot a rainbow of lights at our attackers. Screams fill the room. Their shield spell dims before going out entirely. Soon, it's an even fight. At least enough that we can work our way into the room.

As I go toward the closest prisoner, Jack yells, "Be careful."

"You too."

I slam a hex into the last warlock between the prisoner and me. The warlock falls to the ground, completely asleep. I jump over him, put a shield at my back, and work on the woman's lock. It's not complicated to pick with magic. The complicated part is her condition. As soon as I unlock her, she falls, slumping against me. There's little energy left in her, even less than any of the other prisoners we've encountered.

At this rate, we're going to have to kill or knock out all these warlocks before we can rescue the people. Though the woman is light from her time of torture, the weight is heavy on me. I promised I would come back and save them. I can't go back on that. I can't leave them here a second time.

Suddenly, Jack is at my side, taking the woman from me. "Go get the next one. We'll pass her outside to where they can better help her."

Brilliant idea. I release her, running to the next prisoner as soon as I know Jack has her. I dodge two spells on the way, setting up a shield spell as soon as I get there. As soon as I release the next prisoner, Jack is back at my side. We're making a line between us, the prisoners, and the warlocks, passing the prisoners along as I release them. A second line forms in front of us to help protect them as we pass them along.

Sooner than I would have thought we could do it, the prisoners are all free. Now we just need to get ourselves, and them, away from this place safely. There's not many warlocks left standing at this point. As long as nothing goes wrong, we'll make it.

I join Cynthia's side, attacking the last ten or so warlocks. They are fierce and strong, hence why they are left. A burgundy spell comes out of nowhere and splices my leg open. I hiss in pain and throw a sleep spell back. The warlock puts up a shield spell before it can reach him.

We need another weakness, like the feet from before, but there's nothing left but hardened warlocks. The only consolation is that I don't see a single prisoner in sight. I only hope we don't become the new prisoners.

"Retreat," I call out.

Cynthia gives me a quizzical glance but backs up to the hallway as the rest of them do. Once we're out of sight of the warlocks, I say, "Why don't we bring the building down, like we did to the law office before the rest of you joined us?"

"That was you?" Theodore asks.

I shrug, but inside I'm glowing.

"I think it would work," Jack says.

"It would slow them down at the very least," Tawny says. "That may be enough to get everyone out of here."

"Let's get out of here then so we can bring it down," I reply.

A dark green spell flies over our heads, explodes over us, burning us where the sparks hit. It stings my face and arms.

"Move it," I call out.

Cynthia throws a purple spell behind us as we all file through the hallway. It's too narrow to move fast as we need to. Another spell, yellow this time, comes sailing at us. Before I can react, Theodore casts a shield spell, blocking the attack. It gives the last of us just enough time to escape out into the open.

It'll do no good to bring the building down. The others are already fighting off attackers, the rescued prisoners safely in the middle of them, trying desperately to hold each other up. I ache from the last fight. I don't know how much I or anyone else has left for a fight. But I didn't come here just to be captured. I'll spit on the Grand Chancellor before I'll let the Chardonians capture me.

I run to the front of the line while using my battle cry. Before I even reach the front of the line, I blast out a flurry of sleep spells, trying to hit as many warlocks as I can. Several fall to the ground by the time I reach the front lines. Only, the attackers like my idea

so much, they're flinging sleep spells back at us. One hits a
warlock next to me, but I don't stop until I've reached the front
line, screaming the entire way.

My presence seems to re-energize my group. The rate they
fling spells increases enough that the other side is back off. I turn
toward the back and yell, "Bring the building down!"

I fling several more sleep spells in front of me, aiming toward
the warlocks moving the fastest. There's a crash behind me. The
building is coming down, power lines snapping. One comes flying
our way, landing on the ground between us and the forest of our
escape. I curse under my breath.

"Get away from it," I yell. It could still be live and who knows
how many of these people, especially the women, know about
electricity. One more thing to add to the list to teach them. At
least, after we get out of this mess.

Which gives me an idea. If the two are going to collide, we
might as well make it as full on of a crash as we can. I siphon my
magic toward the downed line. Before my magic reaches it, I will
it to touch the line and shove the energy toward our attackers,
then break off the connections.

"Run," I yell.

Some are already doing so, but at the sound of my voice, the
rest join in, many helping the people we rescued. We go around
the crushed building, making our way around the fallen line, just
as I make it to the building, my spell goes off. Or rather, the
current of electricity slams into the remaining warlocks.

I cringe, wishing it didn't need to come to this, but for now,
we're safe.

CHAPTER 49

Because the people are so weak, it takes over a week to get everyone back to the cave, but there are no further problems with being spotted. It's a near miracle we make it without further delay. Everyone is worn and tired, but I would love to see the Grand Chancellor's face right now. To know how badly we hit him. We should meet with Nathaniel soon to find out how much damage we're really doing, if we're doing any good at all.

Serena and Bethany do a good job of getting the people we rescued settled. Each of them is paired off into a smaller cavern room with at least one other person that was here before. They are weak enough that someone needs to be able to keep an eye on them. A man comes up to me, the one I remember yelling at me the first time we came to come back for them.

"Thank you for saving us."

My cheeks heat. "It wasn't just me. But I'm glad you're here and safe."

"You are doing more than you know."

As he walks off, a voice behind me says, "He's right, you know."

I spin around to find Jack watching me, almost smiling.

"How long have you been standing there?" I ask.

"Long enough to know I'm not the only one who's had a change of heart because of you."

"I've had a lot of help." But my cheeks grow warmer. He leans in, and in front of anyone passing by, kisses my cheek. My face is now flaming, but so is my chest, in the best possible way.

"Katherine sent us both a message," he says.

"Oh?" I try to collect myself.

"It seems you talked her into something."

I grin, knowing exactly what he's talking about. "There's to be a wedding."

"And we're invited."

* * *

EVERYONE WHO MATTERS IS HERE. Katherine and Charles, of course. Jack, Serena, Tawny, Cynthia, Lukas, Bethany, and many tarnished who I don't know. Everyone except Zade.

My heart aches for my brother. I don't just miss him. I need him. There's no one like a brother, and he's been gone far too long. I can't even think on what he must be going through. I have to get him back. No more of this waiting.

At least, not after the wedding.

For now, it's time to celebrate. Time to give Katherine and Charles the moment they deserve. The moment we all need.

We're sitting on the ground, with the couple in the center, a tarnished woman standing next to them. I don't know if this is customary in Chardonia or not, but it's different than our ceremonies. Sitting on the dirt could just be because of the lack of chairs in nature, but the rest I don't know. Or maybe they like to sit in dirt for weddings.

Then again, I don't know what the engagement ceremony was like, but Serena despised it so much she would never talk about it.

Just clams up whenever I bring the topic up. I would think wedding ceremonies would be the same. Maybe here and now they are beginning a new tradition. A new way of marrying two people.

Charles and Katherine look so happy, beaming at each other. They are different too. Never before have I seen a tarnished get married. Katherine is still shaving her head, tattoos across both her and Charles' faces. It's so much a part of them. I only notice when I stop to think about it. Both are wearing nice clothes but not spelled like an Envadi's would be. Simple dark green breeches and white shirts for them both. Elegant material made up simply, but beautifully.

"Does anyone have any words of wisdom for the bride and groom before we start?" the tarnished woman next to them says, her voice clear. It's harder to tell because of her tarnished state, but she looks older, like she might have gray hair if she still had hair. She's dressed in bright colors, an orange skirt and a bright pink shirt.

No one says anything. Even if I could think of something, I'd remain silent. All my advice can be given in private. Not that I have any more to give now that she's taken my advice to get married. That's the best I could do.

"Never take advantage of having each other," Serena says, her voice cracking with emotion. "Enjoy each moment."

I swipe away the tears that trickle down. Serena would know better than anyone else just how important those words are. I scoot closer to Jack, wishing it could be any other way.

"Charles," a male tarnished says, "Remember that your wife is always right."

There's a small amount of laughter through the crowd. Not enough to break the peace of the moment, but enough to bring back the spirit of happiness.

"Always say you're sorry when you've made a mistake," a

female tarnished says. "No matter how small, you'll be happier in the long run if you admit your wrong doings and work to fix them."

"Never go to bed angry," a female tarnished says.

"Tell him exactly what you're feeling and thinking, Katherine," a male tarnished says. "Us men can be dull-witted when it comes to guessing. You need to spell it out for us."

Katherine's grin grows at this as she gives him a nod.

Silence follows.

"Doe anyone else have any words to add?" the standing tarnished asks.

No one speaks up.

"Well then, as mother of the groom," there are several gasps from the tarnished, "I think it's only fitting I do so."

Katherine's grin beams even brighter as she looks at her future mother-in-law.

"Cherish each other," the tarnished woman continues. "No matter what's to come, take care of one another and value each moment you have together. Have you any words for each other?"

Katherine leans forward and whispers something in Charles's ear. He kisses her on the cheek and the replies in a voice lower than we can hear. The two look so perfect together, happy and wonderful as they share words meant only for them.

Jack grabs my hand. I glance up at him, surprise reverberating through me. Who knew such a tough guy could be a romantic? I lean toward him, resting my head on his shoulder as the ceremony continues. Peace settles through me, more than I've felt in the years since I've come to Chardonia. I'm surprised to realize, I'm content.

"May we all remember this day," the woman says, "the love of this couple and strive to spread its warmth throughout all of Chardonia."

The thought strengthens me, making me want to do what she

says. To share this bright light burning inside me. To help others see like Jack has seen. We may be making war with the Grand Chancellor, but we're bringing kindness and love to everyone else. Like all those we've saved from power plants, hunger, and torture.

We've all done much more than we thought we could.

CHAPTER 50

The wedding is a memory I will always cherish, but we can't linger on it. There's a war to plan.

"I think we're ready," I say to the core group of leaders. "We need to attack now that we've weakened key players and places."

"Do you really think we can win this?" Annabelle asks.

"Maybe," Theodore says. "If we do it right."

"We will win," I say, hope a bright flame inside me.

"She's right," Jack says. "I think now would be the best time to attack the Grand Chancellor's home."

"We need to attack with everything we have."

"Don't you think it's a little dangerous to be putting everything we have into this one battle? If we lose—" Bethany says.

"We won't lose," Chadwick says. "Not if we put everything we have into it."

Serena replies, "But if we do, there's more than just us at stake."

I put an arm around her. "Which is why we have to win."

"And we can win," Tawny says. "It won't be easy, but we can do it. We will bring down the Grand Chancellor."

"I'm scared," Bethany says.

I move to her side and slip my arm around her like I just did to

Serena. "I know. I am too. I think we all are. But this is something we can take on. Something we're past ready to do. We can't let the Grand Chancellor go on ruling the country the way he has been."

She lets out a shaky breath and nods.

"She's right," Jack says. "We can win this if everyone is behind us. We can finally put an end to the Grand Chancellor's tyranny."

"How do we win?" Annabelle, sounding resigned.

"Let me go over the plan," I reply, eager to finally put it in the works.

* * *

"ARE YOU READY FOR THIS?" I ask Serena, Cynthia, Tawny, and Bethany.

Bethany's eyes are wide as if she's still scared, but she nods. It's just as well. I'm scared, too.

"More than ready," Cynthia says.

"Honestly," Serena says. "I'm frightened. It's going to be a dangerous job, but it needs to be done."

"Agreed." I try not to bite my nails. It's a habit I've never gotten into, and I'm not about to start now.

"I'm past ready," Tawny says. "If my people knew how bad this was, they'd be here at our side. At least more than are already here."

"Your people?" Serena questions.

"She means our people." I give Tawny a look. "The Envadi. Just think how wonderful it would be to see the faces of those with the Grand Chancellor if a bunch of *barbarians* were joining you in the attack."

"That would scare them good." Serena smiles. "I remember how scared I was the first time I saw Zade." Her grin fades.

"We'll get to him," I say. "We'll get there, and he'll be just as safe as can be. Only bored out of his mind from sitting around so long and thrilled to see us."

She nods, but the doubt in her eyes matches the doubt in my heart. I don't know that the Grand Chancellor would really just let him sit around. But I've learned more about healing than I used to know. As soon as I can, I'll heal him up as best I can. If we can get him good enough to go home, we'll buy him the best healers in Envado. I only hope his injuries aren't too severe. I hold onto that thought. The Grand Chancellor wanted to show off his death at the next tournament. He has to have left him in good enough shape to be there.

And maybe my fears are wrong. Maybe the Grand Chancellor is treating him better than I thought. Unlikely though it may be, maybe there is reason to hope.

We're silent after that, all lost in our own thoughts, fears, and hopes. Time passes, what seems like an infinite amount of time, but it does move. Eventually, Lukas comes for Cynthia. They are darling together. But from the look in Serena's eye, I know she's missing Zade. They should have been married by now instead of being separated by a sadistic lunatic.

"We'll see him soon," I whisper to her.

Her mouth pinches together like she's trying to keep from crying out, but she nods. It takes several hours to form a plan of attack. One I hope will win us the day, but with backup plans in case it doesn't. With any luck, we'll be seeing Daniel and Zade in the near future.

CHAPTER 51

This is it. It's finally time to take down the Grand Chancellor. We will not just meet him on his own territory, but we will smash him. And then, we'll save Zade and Daniel.

There's no hiding this time. No cowering behind bushes or running from guards. It's just us, straight up, ready to attack. We're numbered many more than the guards and servants the Grand Chancellor keeps. With a little help from Nathaniel on the inside, the Grand Chancellor isn't going to know what hit him.

I'm in the front of the line at the Grand Chancellor's house, ready, next to Jack. To one side is Cynthia, Lukas, Chadwick, Katherine, and Charles. Those two are the only tarnished present. On the other side of me are Serena and Annabelle, the former with a gun in hand, and both with the fierce look of a determined warrior on their faces. I would not want to be the person standing between them and those they love. It will be dire.

No holding back. No waiting for an attack. It's just us, ready to charge ahead.

"Before we do this," Jack says for my ears alone. "I want you to know something."

"What is it?"

"I think I've fallen in love with you."

"And I think I've fallen in love with you."

I don't know who starts the kiss first. We both move toward each other like we're the only thing in the world, and we won't let anything stop us from being together. From kissing.

His lips are on mine, and I kiss him back with all the energy and feelings I have for him. It moves through me, filling me with peace even amidst the war. But the peace quickly turns into something more. A blaze building through me. Consuming me. It's like being in the midst of thousands of firework spells, all reaching toward a grand finale more spectacular than any before it.

When our lips finally part, it's with great hesitance. I'd much rather go on kissing him then do what needs to be done. But we are needed.

As the world comes back into focus, those around us are grinning at us. But it doesn't last. Not now. Not when blood is what's to come.

We grab hands, and I savor the final moments we may have together. Our group must have finally been noticed from the inside because the guard is spreading out on the front lawn.

"Let's go to war," I call out.

Behind us, the world fills with war cries. The type of war cries that say they've never been to war before, but they're ready to give all they have for a freedom that's been ripped from them. A freedom we're about to take back.

I step forward, and the others follow. All six hundred of them. There's only a few who aren't here, like Phyllis who refused to come and Pernilla who's taking care of the babies. Everyone else is a group of rage at what's been done to them. The moment we've worked toward, the freedom I've wanted for Chardonia, is about to finally happen.

As we move forward, so do the guards. My spell is the first to fly, a bright yellow splattered with orange fury, like a lightning bolt across their front lines. Some of the guards block it with different types of spells. Others do not, getting zapped with the bolt of electricity.

Spells are flying all around now, a plethora of deadly colors. Someone cries out behind me, but even more cry out in front of me. The battle pricks my heart, making me ache for the guards who defend the Grand Chancellor. If only they wouldn't support him, we wouldn't have to fight them.

"On your left," Tawny cries out.

I throw a hastily shield together on my left side just in time for a burgundy spell to smash against it. Hexes continue to fling toward our group, but not as many as we're sending out. The battlefield is an array of colors, reds blues, purples, blacks, yellows, every color I can think of, and more are stretching toward us and our enemy.

I think we're winning. Nathaniel said these would be the only guards. If we can just get past them, we'll only have the Grand Chancellor to deal with. The thought spurs me on. I flash a burgundy spell, filled with rage at how the Chardonians have been treated. The spell hits a guard who falls to the ground and doesn't get back up.

The guards are growing few and far between. We're making headway toward the house. We've got this. We're winning the battle. Soon, victory will be ours.

Quiet descends. Not a peaceful sort of silence, but one that leaves a chill in the air. The guards who have not fallen part and move to their knees. If it weren't for the parting, I would think they are surrendering. But this is no surrender. They are honoring someone. There's only one someone that could be.

The Grand Chancellor.

CHAPTER 52

Moments later, the Grand Chancellor strides out onto the field, Chancellor Ryan on one side, Chancellor Stephen on the other.

"I want my son," Stephen shouts.

How did he know? I glance at the girls, all of whom have gone pale.

"You only have daughters," Cynthia yells.

"Not anymore. And I want him. Now."

We must have a spy in our midst. How else would Stephen know? We've known all along it was a possibility. But who would possibly betray us. Phyllis. One of the few people who refused to come fight. Of course it's her. Only it's Theodore that steps forward. "Your son is back at their hiding spot in the caves with the mother and daughters. I'll take you to him if you promise my safety."

Immediately, I want to zap the traitor with a hex. To think I healed him. "How could you?" I yell.

He smirks at me. "You didn't really think I'd want to free a bunch of women, did you?"

Stupidly, I did.

"You have a deal," Stephen says, ignoring me.

The traitor walks over to join the Chancellors and Grand Chancellor. I want to hex all three of them with the most powerful spell I have. But the way the Grand Chancellor carries himself like he has no fear of our entire rebellion stays my hand. Why does he not fear us? Or…is it possible? Could he be about to surrender to us?

But then why is he grinning?

He raises his hands, and I just barely have time to throw a shield up before a black with crimson and gold streaked spell flies at our entire group. It slams against my protective spell with a burst of black, darkening my world.

My power wanes fighting against his, becoming weak inside me. I need rest. We all need rest.

The Grand Chancellor smiles, a viscous, hungry smile that says he wants all our deaths. He holds both arms out to the side, and his Chancellors step forward, one on either side of him.

My throat chokes up, but at least he's sending Ryan and Stephen, though I can't help but wonder how the girls will handle fighting against their own father, even if he is a jerk.

Several hexes fling our way, crimson light smashing against our shields. I shove a cutting spell out, straight at Stephen. His shield is thrown up a little too late, leaving cuts on his arms.

Ryan spits a hex out, glittering with red and black. It's headed straight for me. I don't have enough energy left for a shield. No time to move. Then something slams into me, knocking me to the ground with a painful thud.

Chadwick lays next to me, groaning. He just saved me from Chancellor Ryan. Ryan! I jump to my feet and cast a vicious burgundy hex toward his heart. It misses, hitting the side of his shield instead. He laughs and aims his hand at me.

Cynthia flashes a black spell straight at Chancellor Ryan. It smashes into him, and the whole field goes silent as he falls to the ground.

I run to Chadwick, his leg twisted wrong. He coughs.

"Just hang on. I'll heal you right up."

He coughs again, this time with some blood. "It's too late for me."

"No, it can't be!"

He puts a hand on my cheek before I can start to heal him, drawing my gaze to his. "Be happy with Jack. He'll treat you well."

"But you have to stick around to fight with me." My tears run onto his hand.

"I love you."

His hand goes slack. I check his pulse.

Nothing.

Chadwick is dead.

CHAPTER 53

The world grows dark. Cold. Without Chadwick, it will never be the same. Zade will be beside himself when he finds out his best friend died to save me. I want to shrivel up into a ball and never come out. But there's not time to think of it. The Grand Chancellor is raging toward Cynthia.

She stares him down like he's nothing more than a bug in her way.

He raises his hands, but before he can cast a spell, Nathaniel comes running out of the house. "Wait! Father, wait!"

He runs right up to the Grand Chancellor like he doesn't care that he's the most powerful man in the county, maybe even the world.

"You can't harm them."

"What?" The Grand Chancellor's voice is low, but threatening.

"They are just trying to get their freedom. You can't hurt them over that."

"You should be out here helping me, not stopping me."

"But—"

The Grand Chancellor throws a silver spell at his own son.

Someone nearby gasps as Nathaniel is raised in the air, wrapped in that silver spell, and flown back into the house out of sight.

The Grand Chancellor turns back to us, his expression disturbingly calm. "I don't tolerate disobedience. Not from anyone."

A spell the color of an angry cloud flies from him. Cynthia blocks it as best she can, while we help. Tawny is too close to the battle. Too close to the Grand Chancellor. The Queen is going to have my head and hers. If the Grand Chancellor doesn't get us first.

My power is so weak. Faint. No one else must be doing much better as another spell crashes into our shield. The pure wall cracks.

"Retreat," I call, heart heavier than our loss.

As one, we move backward, working to escape while still maintaining the spell. The spell grows weaker. As I look around, I realize that not everyone retreating is interested in helping us all retreat. They're already gone.

My power is weak. So, so weak. And though Cynthia is stronger than me, she can't be doing much better after this fight. "We have to go."

Cynthia nods.

"Run," I say.

We all turn and run.

CHAPTER 54

My legs ache with the movement. Around us, people are falling to the ground, but there's no stopping to help them if we want to make it out of this alive. Jack's suddenly at my side, arm around me, pushing me forward.

"Faster," he yells.

We meet Lukas up ahead in the forest, and he springs the trap as soon as we cross. Us, the last ones left standing that hadn't already made it out.

The trap was a backup plan. Something we should have never had to use. And yet, here it is, whistling up in bright colors. It should make anyone who tries to cross it fall asleep and do the same thing to any spells crossing it's path, making them heavy and slow until the spell wears off, long enough for us to get away.

We keep running, eager to be away from this place. My body is bruised and broken from the fight but not nearly as bad as my heart. How could we have failed so miserably? At least we're safe for now. Those of us still alive, that is. I glance back to make certain the trap is doing its job.

It's not.

"The Grand Chancellor has broken through it," I yell, panic overwhelming me.

The best we can do now is keep running.

Cynthia zaps a few spells behind us as we go, a track-erasing spell, a wall spell. Lukas adds a few of his own. I want to add something, but I'm so drained, I don't think anything would help at all. At least they can offer something to slow the Grand Chancellor down. They must slow him down enough, because he doesn't appear in sight.

We run and run and run. We keep going until my lungs are on fire and my legs burn. When we can't run anymore, we change to a hurried walk, followed by more running. We put several miles of forest between us and the house.

"Are we far enough yet?" I gasp out.

"I don't..." Serena gasps out as well, "think we'll ever be far enough."

My heart burns with how true that statement is.

* * *

AFTER MORE RUNNING than I have ever done in my life, we make it to a far off clearing and don't see any signs of being followed, so we head home. Or to what used to be home. I'm thinking with this new fall of our rebellion, that's going to have to change.

"Is everyone here? Who's missing?" I say.

There are many from the six hundred that are missing. More than I want to think on. Nelly among them. I can only hope she's somewhere else and not dead or captured.

Other than Chadwick and the treacherous Theodore, our group of leaders seems to be coming together. Except, "Where's Tawny?"

"I haven't seen her," Jack says.

"Neither have I," Cynthia replies.

Sick dread weighs down my heart as I remember seeing her on

the field too close to the actions. I fall to a sitting position, ending on the ground. I have lost one of the heirs to the throne. She's probably dead.

My heart aches as I begin to cry. It's all too much. I wanted this war to save lives, to save an entire people. Instead, I've lost more than everyone had to begin with. I have utterly failed not just myself, and the crown, but all of Chardonia.

Someone puts a hand on my shoulder. I glance up to find Jack, his own eyes filled with tears. We have lost everything.

CHAPTER 55

After some time, I pull myself together. I have to do what I can for the people left. After all, we have a traitor who is probably, even now, telling them where we are.

"I think we should have everyone we can moved to Envado." I say to those left. But I know what that decision means. Know who we're leaving behind. My words are clogged with tears. "I don't want to, but I think it would be for the best."

Serena is crying now, even harder than I am. "We can't leave Zade. We can't do it."

My own tears come harder, the ache in my chest a giant hole of agony. "We have to."

Cynthia and Bethany gather us both in a hug, tears on both their cheeks as well.

"We'll try again," I say. "We won't just leave him there. We'll try again and again until we get him out."

"We will," Serena says, though it almost sounds more like a question.

"We will. Somehow, we'll make it so you two can have that wedding you've been waiting for."

Her tears slow as she brushes them away, and she nods.

"Now, to the cave so we can start evacuating people to Enva-do," Cynthia says.

"To Envado," I say. To my home that's no longer home but all I have left.

CHAPTER 56

I t's dark and lonely just outside the cavern. I can't bring myself to go in, though. To face my failure. To know lives were lost because I pushed us to go. Loneliness seems a small repayment for that but not nearly enough of one to make up for Chadwick.

My chest gives a painful squeeze. How can he really be gone?

"What are you doing out here all alone?" Jack asks.

His company is already a soothing presence, but one I don't know if I deserve. "Just thinking."

"Anything you'd like to talk about?"

I rest my head on my knees. "I don't know. It's all so jumbled and painful."

"I wish things could have turned out differently."

"Who knew the Grand Chancellor would be more powerful than all of us put together? There's going to be no stopping him."

"Then we'll get away from him."

"But what if he follows us to Envado? What if he tries to take over my country as well?"

"Then we'll have an even bigger group to fight against him, yes?"

I nod. "That is true."

"And sooner or later he's going to take on a group that is too big and powerful for him to handle."

"I only wish that would have been us today."

"So do I."

"How do you feel about Chadwick?" Jack asks.

Those tears start to well again. The last couple of days have been horrid to get through. "Guilty. I think I'll always feel guilty. But grateful too. I'm not ready to go. Something about him, though. He almost seemed ready. He loved me, but knew I could never return those feelings."

"I'm sorry it had to end that way for him. He was a good man."

"The best of men."

Silence descends as I remember him and the life he gave for me.

"He wanted me to be happy, though. He knew that we could never be. That's what he gave me. The ultimate sacrifice so I could live and be happy."

"Do you think you can be happy after his loss?"

"It will take time to mourn him. Not just him, but our loss. Everything we were trying to gain but failed at. Happiness seems like a very distant thing right now."

"I know what you mean," he says. "As far as I've come as a person, I wanted us to come farther as a group. As a nation."

"And yet, here we are, running." I sigh.

"Just think if you weren't here, though. All these people we're getting to Envado. Would that happen without you?"

"Someone else from Envado would lead them."

"But would they have led like you did?"

Lead everyone to failure? Or maybe not. This is a loss. One harder than I know how to deal with. But when I think back on everything that happened. Everything I've accomplished, maybe it's not so much of a failure.

Women know more magic, know what they can do magic. The lower class knows there is a better way of life, even if I couldn't give it to them. Jack is a perfect example of this. He's grown so much, and there's no knowing that someone else would have been able to do that. The people I've helped, the lives I've touched. No knowing at all if someone else could have done it. "I suppose not."

"So you being here might not have turned out like you were expecting, but it's still critical to saving a lot of people's lives."

"When you put it that way…"

"You are great, Waverly."

"I want you to know something," I say, and then take a deep breath, steeling myself to say what needs to be said. "I love you, Jack."

Instantly, his arms are around me, warming me. "I love you too."

And then we're kissing. There's much sorrow and pain in the kiss, but it's healing too. Like all the pain we had knows that love is just what it needs to help it feel better. The kiss deepens, and it's like a flood of emotions pouring through me. I never want it to end.

His fingers tangle in my hair, pulling me closer, and mine tangle in his. Pulled together like this, it feels as if we can do anything. Conquer anything. Win anything. Even if we can't, at least we have the love of each other.

My heart pounds as his lips move with mine. If only it was as easier to heal all our problems as Jack is at healing my heart.

* * *

IT'S time to get us out of here and go to Envado. Everyone else is gone. It's our turn. If it wasn't for the love I have for Jack, and my girls and littlest new baby boy, I'd feel hollow. My chest is threatening to feel hollow anyway. For all we've been through, it just wasn't enough, and we've lost good people during the process. And I still don't have Zade.

None of this was how it's supposed to be. The Grand Chancellor has taken away everything. Our home is no longer safe. The lives we lived were taken away. Our loved ones stolen through imprisonment or death. Our hopes and dreams have been stolen, whisked away by a man more powerful than one man should be.

Other than having each other, nothing is ours.

AFTERWORD

If you enjoyed reading this book, please consider helping the author by leaving a review where you purchased the book and/or on Goodreads.

You can sign up to receive newsletters from Janeal Falor at www.janealfalor.com on the Works in Progress page. Or talk to the author directly at janealfalor@gmail.com

BOOKS BY JANEAL FALOR

Young Adult Fantasy

Mine Series
Mine to Tarnish (Mine Prequel)
You Are Mine (Mine #1)
Mine to Spell (Mine #2)
Mine to Fear (Mine #3)
Sacrifice of Mine (Mine #4)

Death's Queen
Death's Queen (Death's Queen #1)
Death's Betrayal (Death's Queen #2)
Death's Embrace (Death's Queen #3)
Death's Assassin (Death's Queen #4)

Darkening Light
Ever Darkening (Darkening Light #1)
Savage Light (Darkening Light #2)

Elven Princess
Bound by Birthright (Elven Princess #1)
Bound to Endure (Elven Princess #2)
Bound by Love (Elven Princess #3)

Standalone
Goddess Ascending

A Genie's Heart

Fantasy for Adults
Mother of the Chosen
Mother of the Chosen (Mother of the Chosen #1)
Protector of the Chosen (Mother of the Chosen #2)
Guardian of the Chosen (Mother of the Chosen #3)
Sacrifice for the Chosen (Mother of the Chosen #4)

ACKNOWLEDGMENTS

There's so much to be grateful for when a book is complete and this one is no exception. I put a lot of heart and quirkiness into this book. I just love Waverly and the people that helped me make her better.

Thank you to Karen C. Eddington for being not only an incredible sister, but for always helping me make my books better. Lori Hall, thank you for your last minute checking and always being there to bounce thoughts and ideas. I don't know what I'd do without you.

Big thanks to Sarah Canning for reading my work and helping me improve it and for being a friend. Thanks to Sharon Umbaugh for helping me find what I was missing and cleaning things up. Sotia Lazu, thank you for putting up with such a messy rough draft and helping me to turn it into something special.

An overwhelming thanks to my friends and family. Rebecca Webb for encouraging me and being a true friend. Tai, Xandria, and Will for being the most awesome kids ever and always bragging up that mommy's an author. And the biggest thanks to my most amazing husband. I love you!

ABOUT THE AUTHOR

Amazon best selling author Janeal Falor lives in Utah with her husband and three children. In her non-writing time she teaches her kids to make silly faces, cooks whatever strikes her fancy, and attempts to cultivate a garden even when half the things she plants die. When it's time for a break she can be found taking a scenic drive with her family or drinking hot chocolate.

www.ingramcontent.com/pod-product-compliance
Lightning Source LLC
Chambersburg PA
CBHW070105030726
47506CB00002B/597

* 9 7 8 0 9 8 9 7 4 3 2 5 9 *